She was acting like a lovesick schoolgirl.

Maybe if she met Peter socially more often the glow would fade, and she would discover he was just a mere mortal with ordinary failings, like any other human being. In fact, she had thought just that when he had been so cutting about Nadja, but the trouble was she so quickly forgave him, and then the attraction crept back again. . .

CW00796821

Kids. . .one of life's joys, one of life's treasures.

Kisses. . .of warmth, kisses of passion, kisses from mothers and kisses from lovers.

In *Kids & Kisses*. . .every story has it all.

Frances Crowne's nursing career was set aside for marriage and three children, yet left a sense of thwarted ambition. Later a secretarial career at an agricultural college was followed by freelance writing of romantic fiction and articles for women's magazines. A chance remark at a party led to her writing her first medical stories. Now woven with romance, her nursing ties have come full circle in a most gratifying way.

Recent titles by the same author:

SUNLIGHT AND SHADOW
LOVING QUEST
LOVE'S CASUALTIES

DR WENTWORTH'S
BABIES

BY
FRANCES CROWNE

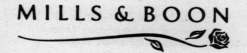

MILLS & BOON

DID YOU PURCHASE THIS BOOK WITHOUT A COVER?
If you did, you should be aware it is **stolen property** as it was
reported *unsold and destroyed* by a retailer. Neither the Author
nor the publisher has received any payment for this book.

*All the characters in this book have no existence outside the imagina-
tion of the author, and have no relation whatsoever to anyone bearing
the same name or names. They are not even distantly inspired by any
individual known or unknown to the author, and all the incidents are
pure invention.*

*All rights reserved. The text of this publication or any part thereof
may not be reproduced or transmitted in any form or by any means,
electronic or mechanical, including photocopying, recording, storage
in an information retrieval system, or otherwise, without the written
permission of the publisher.*

*This book is sold subject to the condition that it shall not, by way
of trade or otherwise, be lent, resold, hired out or otherwise circulated
without the prior consent of the publisher in any form of binding or
cover other than that in which it is published and without a similar
condition including this condition being imposed on the subsequent
purchaser.*

MILLS & BOON, the Rose Device and
LOVE ON CALL are trademarks of the publisher.
*Harlequin Mills & Boon Limited,
Eton House, 18-24 Paradise Road, Richmond, Surrey TW9 1SR
This edition published by arrangement with Harlequin Enterprises B.V.*

© Frances Crowne 1995

ISBN 0 263 79394 X

*Set in Times 10 on 11 pt. by
Rowland Phototypesetting Limited
Bury St Edmunds, Suffolk*

03-9511-51046

*Made and printed in Great Britain
Cover illustration by Alexis Liosatos*

CHAPTER ONE

THE London to Scotland express train sped smoothly across the borders into the Scottish countryside on that bright, cold March day, intermittent sunshine causing giant cloud shadows to form against the towering hills. Laura Meadows was intrigued by the scenic view as she gazed out from the window; this was the moment she had waited for ever since leaving King's Cross, London. Nevertheless, it would have been more exciting but for the recollection of her air-steward boyfriend's voice still ringing in her ears. He had been furious when she had told him she was taking on a new job.

'Inverness?' he'd exploded. 'Why the hell are you going up north? And what about us?' he'd added churlishly, eyes cold.

Laura had had a great urge to laugh. It was only then she had realised how at times he reminded her of a small boy in a sweet shop who expected to have everything he saw just when he wanted it.

'Keith, I've already told you, I'm not sharing that flat of yours near Heathrow in the vain hope that you'll arrive just some time. The affair was OK while it lasted, but now we're through. For heaven's sake let's be realistic. . .'

She stared out at the majestic peaks protecting small, isolated farmsteads, gushing rivers foaming happily on their way to the sea, long, dark green tracts of pine forest, silent and mysterious. This part of the country was still unknown to her and she was determined to enjoy it; there was an air of freshness and energy about

5

it. With a small sigh of relief and contentment, she pushed back a tress of her long fair hair and settled down to read a paperback. She was actually beginning to feel a new sense of freedom. And why not, at twenty-six?

Soon people began to move up and down the aisle of the carriage bringing refreshments back and forth from the buffet car. Thinking of doing the same, she was about to stand up when a girl around her own age, suddenly lurched towards her as the train swung round a curve in the track, narrowly preventing the contents of the beaker she carried going over the dark green jacket of Laura's suit.

The girl looked mortified as she straightened up and grabbed the back of the seat. 'Oh, I'm so sorry; did the coffee spill on to you?'

Laura laughed. 'No, it's OK. One of the penalties of an outside seat, I suppose! I booked rather late.'

The girl glanced at her conspiratorially. 'Look, there's a window seat opposite me if you'd like to move back there. The woman who reserved it has already gone.'

'Oh, great! Thanks, I will.'

'I'll take one of your bags if you like and lead on.'

They settled comfortably into their seats, Laura's luggage stowed near by. 'Phew! This is heaps better.' She grinned thankfully.

'I'm Gemma Sinclair, by the way,' the girl smiled, her madcap mop of brown curls enhancing round brown eyes.

'Hi! I'm Laura—Laura Meadows. I really appreciate your help.'

'Pleasure. I've been going nearly mad not talking to anyone; the other three passengers with me here were tucked behind books most of the time. Are you going through to Inverness?'

'Yes.'

'That's good, me too. Only about another three hours or so to go now. I think I'll just nip back and buy a snack; didn't think of it when I was juggling with the coffee. Is there anything I can get you?'

'Could you manage another coffee, do you think?'

'Nothing to it!'

Laura was glad of the girl's company, and when she returned found they had quite a lot to talk about in general: clothes, hair, make-up, travel, boyfriends; even a ten-minute stop at Edinburgh almost went by unnoticed.

Gemma was staring out at the passing scene when she said unexpectedly, 'Do you know, Laura, I'm supposed to be getting married in the autumn? But I'm not sure if I love Ken enough.'

'How long have you known him?'

'On and off most of our lives. Our parents have been good friends ever since we were born, really. We went to the same schools, even went on holiday together with our families. I love Ken, but sometimes he seems more like a brother to me—do you know what I mean? At times I feel as if I don't know much about life at all. . .' She bit her lip suddenly. 'Sorry, I shouldn't be telling you all this.' She grinned. 'They say it's easier to talk to strangers because you'll never meet again!'

'I know what you mean, though. There's always some problem or other to work out, isn't there?'

'With those violet eyes of yours, I bet you've got a regular boyfriend, haven't you?'

'No, we packed it in just a short while ago. He was getting on my nerves. For six months we'd been going out together off and on, but with his job on the airlines I just never knew when I was going to see him. He seemed to think I should rearrange my life to suit his.

It just couldn't be done. Anyway, I didn't see why I should. When I refused to share his flat, that was it, I'm afraid.'

'Yes,' Gemma said thoughtfully. 'Well, at least you've made a stand, and know what you want and don't want. My problem is I've never yet had a choice.' She shrugged. 'Still, I ought not to grumble, I suppose. Ken's a nice enough guy, really. He's at police training college hoping to become a detective. He says he likes a quiet life when he's at home!' She looked troubled, briefly. 'Thing is,' she said with a wry grin, 'I don't know what our parents would do if we changed our minds. They've never stopped talking about the wedding plans!'

'I can imagine.' Laura smiled sympathetically, yet thinking of her own parents in quite a different context, with a divorce pending. Ever since her twenty-four-year-old brother had been killed in a road accident they had been at each other's throats as to whose fault it was for allowing him to have a motorbike. Her home no longer seemed the place it used to be, which was another reason why she wanted the new job. She looked up suddenly, aware of a change of speed.

'I think we're getting into Inverness already,' Gemma said as the train slowly approached the terminus.

'Heck, we must have talked a lot, Gemma. It's been great meeting you, though.'

Gemma was collecting her things together. 'It certainly has; I have a feeling there's still masses we haven't touched upon yet, too.' The train slid to a halt. 'What about exchanging addresses? Maybe we could meet up some time?'

Laura collected her suitcases. 'I don't live here. . .'

'Oh,' Gemma grinned. 'I don't know why I thought you did. Neither do I, as a matter of fact!' They both joined the queue and made their way from the train and through the ticket barrier. 'Somebody's supposed to be meeting me here; I'm going to a new job.'

Laura glanced at her quickly. 'It wouldn't be the Lodge, would it? You're not a nurse?'

Gemma dropped her cases and flung her arms around Laura. 'Yes, on both counts! Thank heavens I've found a pal!'

Laura grinned happily. 'I might have known! There's something about our lot, isn't there?'

It didn't take long for the two girls to spot a young man wearing a deerstalker hat, a scarf flung casually round his neck over his tweeds, smiling broadly at them both while holding up a large white card with 'Lodge Hospital' written on it. 'Good evening, ladies. You are. . .?'

'Laura Meadows.'

'Gemma Sinclair.'

'I'm Dennis—Dennis McKay. Let's have your bags; the mini-bus is outside; there's plenty of room if you'd like to get in. We just have to wait for one more. . .' He looked at his list. 'Let's see, Barnard—Mrs Joan Barnard.'

Gemma and Laura climbed into the van and settled into their seats. 'I think I've got butterflies,' Gemma said suddenly.

'I don't feel so good myself. Supposing this place is like a prison? I mean, we're going to be miles from anywhere. . .'

'This might well be one of the wardresses.'

Apprehensively they watched Dennis welcome a short, rotund lady with a no-nonsense look about her that did not seem to bode well. Her face was long and thin and she wore gold-rimmed spectacles, with short and straight iron-grey hair that did not stir in the rather fierce wind blowing in off the waters of the Moray

Firth. The door of the van opened and Dennis introduced her. 'This is Joan Barnard.'

'Good evening!' they chorused.

'Gemma Sinclair, Laura Meadows,' Dennis beamed. 'Right. Now we can all be on our way.'

The three made desultory conversation about the weather, then fell silent until Joan Barnard said in a clipped, authoritative voice to the two girls, 'I can see I'll be the oldest member of staff, but they said at my interview that wouldn't matter.'

'Why should it, Joan?' Laura said in an effort to be friendly. 'I expect you've had lots of experience in the job; nursing these days offers so much variety.'

'You can say that again,' Gemma joined in. 'Getting to be a staff nurse was hard enough, but I'm willing to keep struggling!'

'Me too,' Laura added. 'I've done a paediatrics course as well. I'm hoping the Lodge will give me some more practical aspects of it.'

'It should do, Laura,' Gemma said with a grin. 'Apparently they're taking in children, preferably from international war zones. Poor little devils, they're bound to be in a bad state. Jolly interesting for us, though. What do you do in the hierarchy, Joan?'

Joan Barnard gave Gemma a brief glance, her expressionless face grey and tired. 'Oh, me, I'm an FRCS,' she said offhandedly. 'You'll have to excuse me for not talking too much; I've been travelling since yesterday morning.'

Gemma and Laura gave each other a look. A Fellow of the Royal College of Surgeons. They would have more to say about their travelling companion later on. . .

Dennis suddenly called from the driving seat, 'And, not wanting to be left out, I'm a charge nurse.'

'Well done, Dennis!' Gemma shouted, giving him a

slap on the back. 'Now that we all know each other, we'll go to sleep!'

'Wouldn't if I were you; we've only another few miles to go.'

It was a black evening, no moon, but with a mass of stars scattered about the sky. The only sign of habitation was an occasional light in a farmhouse, and just once the headlamps of a car passed them in the opposite direction. When they slowed down it was into a short driveway, at the end of which was the large bulk of the Lodge, well-lit and welcoming. They stopped outside a formidable oak and brick entrance, when a sturdy oak-panelled door was flung open, and a smiling young girl stood at the top of a short flight of white stone steps. Within seconds the familiar uniformed figure of a senior nursing officer joined her.

Dennis, in his bright, cheerful manner, introduced them all to Katherine Menzies, her light brown eyes twinkling with pleasure. 'Hello there; how nice to meet you! Do come in. Mary——' she turned to the young girl helping Dennis with the luggage and coats '——just get the coffee now, dear, and we'll have it in my office.'

Seated around a log-burning fire, the travellers welcomed the refreshments Mary brought in. 'This is great, Miss Menzies,' Gemma said warmly. 'We got rather tired of British Rail sandwiches, didn't we, Laura?'

'Yes, but it was a good journey on the whole.' Laura noticed Joan Barnard's eyes drooping with the warmth of the fire as tiredness claimed her. 'I think poor Mrs Barnard's had a much worse time than us, though, with all her travelling.'

The SNO stood up. 'Just what I was thinking. Now, if you like to come along with me, Joan, we can get you settled into your little flat. I'm sure the nurses

won't mind.' She smiled at them both. 'I'll see you
when I come back.'

Dennis supplied the answer to the question that was
obvious by their expressions. 'Miss Menzies is great
to work for. The place has only been ready such a
short time, none of us has been here for more than a
fortnight, yet she's done wonders.'

'Are there any patients in yet?'

'Oh, yes. We've had one ambulance plane in
already. We took eight and the rest went on to
Inverness.'

Miss Menzies returned then, her face concerned.
'Mrs Barnard has been working in Palestine, you know.
A friend of hers who contacted me, unbeknown to
her, suggested she come to us just to give her a break
from all the dangers she's encountered in the last two
years. A wonderful doctor, from what I can gather.'

She looked at her two new nurses, both trying desperately hard to appear alert, and gave them a smile.
'Come along, you two, I'll take you both upstairs. You
have a rather nice room each in the residential wing,
and I'll tell you all the rules we live by in the morning.'

Laura was far too tired to notice the large, airy,
comfortable room she was shown to, except to feel a
pang of delight that she had a miniature bathroom all
to herself. The wonderfully spacious bed was the only
other thing that got through to her befuddled mind.
After that she remembered nothing more.

It was the tapping on wood that startled her into wake-
fulness. Laura sat bolt upright in the strange bed.
Where on earth was she? The door opened partially,
then everything flooded back. 'Come in, Mary!'

The girl put down a tray of tea with a smile. 'Morning, Nurse. Miss Menzies always spoils her nurses on
their first day here, but after that there's a kettle over

there on the table where you can make your own. Breakfast is in the servery at eight o'clock, but nine today for you new ones.'

Laura pushed back her thick fair hair with a groan, violet eyes sleepy. 'Oh, thanks, Mary, you're a love.'

When the door closed she sat back on her pillows, relishing the tea, then remembered Gemma and wondered how she had fared overnight. For herself she had slept deeply, and was now full of enthusiasm to see everything about the Lodge and meet the people here. She put her cup and saucer aside as there was another tap on the door, and Gemma popped her head round it. 'Hi! Can I come in?'

'Sure. Sit on the bed here. How did you sleep?'

'Not too well at first. About one o'clock this morning I found my way downstairs to the kitchen, and who should I see but Dennis just as I was rummaging around to make a cuppa!'

'Oh, heck, what did he say?'

'He's OK. He was on night duty. Apparently he'd volunteered to meet us first at the station, then went straight on duty. They're short of a driver and general factotum as yet. Dennis seems a nice guy; he told me all about this place and how lucky we are to be here. This is one of several shooting lodges, as well as thousands of acres, owned by the local duke. He and the Duchess are nice, unassuming people who wanted to help and generously allocated one of the lodges to be taken over as a hospital. They often come over here to see how we're getting on.'

'Interesting. Did he say any more about Miss Menzies?'

'Only that, like all SNOs, she's great so long as you don't get on the wrong side of her!' Gemma stood up. 'Well, I'd better go and have my shower. I gather you slept?'

'Like a log, thanks.'

'OK. See you in the servery.'

From then on the day was full of sights, sounds and lingering impressions. To Laura the glorious spread of hills around the gleaming waters of Loch Brora, stretching out before them from every window, was a sight she was sure she would never tire of.

The Lodge itself was built with four gables in solid red brick, framed with broad oak beams giving an almost Elizabethan touch. Its rooms were large, with high, decorative ceilings; ornate staircases swept up to two further storeys with rooms once used for the rich and pampered, all now redecorated and refurbished.

But the interior work still retained an air of grandeur that could not be disguised, and neither did the people brought in to create the change-over want it any other way, the Duke and Duchess having been delighted with the tasteful and creative transformation that had taken place. It was just what they'd hoped for.

The SNO continued their tour after lunch. The three of them gathered in the large panelled reception area, which also included six examination cubicles for casualties. 'There's a lot of good quality equipment here,' Katherine Menzies was saying. 'We have three operating theatres upstairs we'll be looking at later. Are there any questions at this stage?'

Joan Barnard, who was looking more rested, but still with an air of gloom about her, said, 'How many wards have we in use at present?'

'Six, each capable of taking four to six beds and fitted out with all we need at present. In an emergency we could take twenty-four to thirty people——'

Miss Menzies' intercom buzzed. 'Yes, right away.' She glanced at her fob-watch. 'I'm wanted in my office, so I suggest you make your way now to the staff common-room for tea. We're all very informal here.

Dr Steven Lomax or myself will take you round the wards at eight-thirty tomorrow morning, then we'll decide where each of you will be working.'

Over tea everyone was very friendly. There must have been six or seven other members of staff there, and Laura noticed that Joan Barnard was soon in deep conversation with one of the male doctors and seemed more animated.

Gemma thought the same thing. 'I'm glad to see Mrs Barnard looking more normal now. What do you think she's going to be like?'

'Difficult to tell. . .'

The door opened suddenly and a medium-height, thick-set, white-coated doctor of about fifty, with deep blue eyes and thick sandy hair, entered, his long, rather lugubrious face looking round at them as he raised a hand.

'Sorry to interrupt your tea, everyone. Word has it there's likely to be another plane in tomorrow from Eastern Europe. So if it's true just make sure that those who can get a good night's sleep—because you may not be so lucky tomorrow night!'

A brief smile crossed his well-worn features. 'This might only be hearsay but I happened to be passing the SNO's office door just now and overheard part of her telephone conversation. Miss Menzies will be telling you all later, no doubt, but a wee bit of advance information never hurt anybody, ye ken, so don't say I didn't warn you!'

Someone called jokily, 'You're a great one for the doom and gloom, Steven. We'll believe you; thousands wouldn't! I was going out for a pint tonight too!'

Steven Lomax shrugged and stalked out, giving them a wave as he left. The two girls introduced themselves to one or two people then eventually left the common-room, both keen to unpack properly and have an early night after getting their rooms shipshape.

'What about coffee in my room, Gemma, before dinner?' Laura asked once they were upstairs.

'Sure, OK; that'll be great.'

Later, when Gemma returned to Laura's room, she was looking drawn and anxious.

'Hi, Gem, what's wrong?' Laura asked, in the act of filling the pot with ground coffee.

'Oh, honestly, Laura, I don't understand myself! Ken said to ring as soon as I could once I'd arrived and let him know everything was OK. Well, I did just that, going to the phone at the end of the corridor here in case he wanted to ring me back, but when I got through he sounded so flat and uninterested, I wished I hadn't bothered!'

'Why, what did he say?'

'I told him how great it was here; that I'd met you, and I was really happy about everything. And all he said was, "I'm glad to hear it." So, being me, I snapped back with, Is that all you've got to say? He said, "Well, what do you expect me to say when you're all those hundreds of miles away?" Then I said something like, What the devil's up with you? You know I'll be home in three months' time. He practically bit my head off. "Because," he said, "in three months' time I have to go on a course to New York on an exchange thing there."'

Gemma sighed, flopping down on to the bed. 'Anyway, whatever I said made no difference; the pips went then and I'd run out of money so that was that. We didn't even say goodbye.' Tears of frustration welled up in her dark eyes.

'Hey, come on, Gemma, have this cup of coffee! I know what's wrong; he wanted you to be down there with him to tell you all about the course and the fact that he's passed some exam or other. It seems to me men always need to be told how wonderful they are!'

'Yeah.' Gemma managed a grin. 'I reckon you're right, Laura. Actually he *was* taking an exam but never really said much about it or what it was for. Funny, isn't it? There was I drooling over how I'd known him for such a long time and not even sure if I loved him, and now, the minute there's a suggestion he's going away and I'm not his top priority, I suddenly go to pieces!'

Next morning at breakfast in the servery, Miss Menzies announced exactly what Dr Lomax had hinted the day before. Nevertheless, a suitably convincing gasp went up around the tables.

'They should arrive some time between two and four,' she said briskly. 'I'm told I shall hear in good time. Apparently there'll be two male doctors on the plane with the patients—Dr Peter Wentworth—a Scot, I believe—and a Frenchman—Dr Jacques Moreaux. They will be accompanied by two French female nurses; when the hand-over is completed their own responsibility will end and they will fly back to Paris.

'Naturally I expect everyone to be on their toes, and to treat the occasion as our being on full red alert. Thank you, that's all for now.'

Later, Laura was called into Miss Menzies' office. Looking spruce and attractive in her pale lilac and white uniform dress, she listened to what her superior had to say.

'I see from your c.v., Laura, that you were promoted to ward sister at Colchester General until you decided to hand in your notice. I do, of course, remember you telling me all of this on the phone on receipt of your first application for the job, but I needed to refresh my memory! However, as you know, we advertised for staff nurse positions only here, as we're in such a constant state of flux, you understand.

'I intend putting you on Hyacinth twinned with Primrose ward, both of which are surgical, where at present there are two teenage boys and a middle-aged man. I know you're more familiar with paediatric nursing but it's my intention to give most of my nurses all-round experience for the time being so that in the event of another huge demand upon our services in this isolated area you'll be able to cope in a more comprehensive way.

'Now, I don't want you to worry about any of this, but I would ask that you come to me if there are any problems at all. I intend that we be a happy band of people here, which will only work if we're frank and sincere with each other.' She stood up, giving Laura a cursory glance. 'You look very smart in our uniform, so we'll go along to Hyacinth now.'

As staff were still in short supply, when Miss Menzies arrived at the ward there was only one RGN on duty. Miss Menzies made the introductions and left them together. Pearl Oboto was from Nigeria, was tall, elegant and had the most beautiful face Laura thought she had ever seen. Her smile was brilliant, her huge brown eyes like softly glowing lamps.

'Nice to meet you, Staff. As you can see we're not exactly worked off our feet here—yet. But I get the feeling we've quite a few changes coming.'

Laura grinned, looking round at the delightfully airy freshness of the ward, the colourful bed-curtains, light-wood furniture fittings, and above all the picture windows framing the loch and the pale green hills. 'I'm sure you're right, Pearl,' she answered. 'I'd better try and familiarise myself with everything before the onslaught, I think!'

It was at lunchtime that Miss Menzies said that the

incoming patients had landed safely, and would be leaving Inverness in the ambulances provided by the hospital there. A buzz of restrained excitement ensued. Even the patients upstairs on Hyacinth sensed it. The older man on the ward who had had a leg amputation which had been gangrenous by the time he arrived at the Lodge smiled broadly at Laura when Pearl introduced her to him.

'Janek, this is our new staff nurse; she will be looking after you as well.' Pearl spoke slowly, using mostly sign language.

He beamed again, indicating both of them. 'Ah. . . good. . . Very lucky me!' He nodded happily.

'Yes, you are, Janek.' Pearl grinned at Laura as they redid his dressing. 'Most times you are very brave too.'

'Yes, yes,' he nodded.

They made his bed comfortable. 'He's a lovely man,' Pearl told her. 'He hasn't a clue what we're talking about really, but he's picking up a few words fast!'

'Where's he from?' Laura asked, reading his chart.

'Somewhere in Bosnia. If we only had someone here who spoke the language fluently it would make one hell of a difference.'

Laura glanced across at the other two occupied beds. 'Those two seem to be sound asleep.'

'Yes, poor little devils. They're brothers, twins, although you wouldn't think so to look at them. They're so undernourished at the moment, there's nothing we can do for them until we've built up their strength. It's so touching, though—each time they wake up and we go to their bedside, all they do is smile at us. God knows what's really happened to them.'

The telephone shrilled suddenly. Pearl answered it and when she came back she said, 'Miss Menzies is assembling a collection of staff in Reception now. The ambulances should be here at any time. She wants you to go, Laura. I'll remain behind for any instructions.'

Laura felt a sudden frisson of excitement mixed with a slight pang of nervousness as she swiftly made her way down to the meeting point.

CHAPTER TWO

LAURA quickened her steps as she heard someone call, 'Here they come!'

In Reception a ripple of tension was palpable. Laura joined the small gathering of both doctors and nurses waiting to receive people, young and old, who had been rescued from war-torn countries. Laura realised Gemma was at her side, who whispered quickly, 'I'm on the same wards as you; great, isn't it?' Dennis was there too, and Joan Barnard. Miss Menzies was looking calm, yet no doubt anxious to see her next batch of casualties safely settled.

A voice suddenly announced, 'Yes, it is them. Here's the first ambulance!'

From the womb-like warmth of the Lodge, looking through the deep windows, Laura could see ambulances like a string of white beetles on the other side of the loch moving slowly along the foot of the green hills, then as they grew nearer and reached the head of the loch it was possible to see the outline of each vehicle. They drove then more quickly along the arrow-straight path and across the broad plain of springy turf towards the Lodge. With great care they lined up to enter the driveway, crunched slowly over the gravel, then neatly drew up one behind the other to unload.

Miss Menzies looked pleased. 'Excellent. They are in good time. With any luck we should manage to get them all comfortably established before tea.'

'Staff,' she addressed Laura, 'you did tell Dr Lomax that both he and Dr Hudson would be needed here this afternoon, didn't you?'

'Yes, Miss Menzies,' Laura answered, adding suddenly, 'Here they are now.'

'Good. Over here please, Doctors!' She addressed the staff around her. 'Now listen, everyone, remember what I told you. These people have had one hell of a time, especially the children. Firm but loving care is what they need just now. I imagine they hardly know what's happening to them. I know I can rely upon you all to do whatever you can for them.'

The large double doors slid open and the first stretchers were brought in. Labels and ward numbers were ready to be allocated to them. Three very young children began to cry fretfully. They were picked up, clinging to the necks of the two pale-faced nurses with them. The male doctors appeared harassed and tense while handing over the necessary formal papers to Miss Menzies and her secretary.

Laura's heart went out to the men, one of whom was very French, burly, well-built, possibly middle-aged. The other was tall, slim, dark-haired, with a profile almost classic in its handsome aloofness, concentration now etched deeply on his face, making him appear older than the mid-thirties he probably was. He was presently engaged in an intense discussion with Miss Menzies, his voice authoritative, edged with impatience.

'No, it is impossible,' he snapped curtly, on being asked for other papers he obviously did not possess. 'I have already cleared this with both the French and British immigration authorities, and any further documents about these sick people will be provided if and when more information can be collected.' The doctor ran a distraught hand through his fashionable length of sable-black hair, long, sensitive fingers revealing the strain and stress of his mission.

Miss Menzies was quite unperturbed. 'Very well,

Mr Wentworth; we'll sort that out later.'

Nevertheless, the man was not to be outdone, his deep voice commanding as he insisted, 'There is nothing further to add. All I want is to be assured that the adults will not be troubled. Also that the children in particular are not likely to be moved from here because of any needless paperwork!'

Miss Menzies smiled. 'Do not concern yourself, Sir. I will see to it personally that your patients remain with us, unless there is some medical reason why they should have to leave.'

The man murmured his thanks, tiredness and no doubt relief now obvious in the sag of his shoulders. Laura had to admire his persistence as she hurried away again towards the children. This Mr Wentworth was stubborn, she'd say that for him, she thought as the rising cacophony of noise from the five children engulfed her. There were two teenagers, one toddler and two babies under a year old. The little ones were now joining in the hubbub with gusto, their crying even louder above the chatter, to them, of strange tongues, despite drinks and biscuits hurriedly being dispensed by Mary and another helper from the kitchen.

Laura tried soothing the small, dark-eyed girl who seemed determined to scream with no tears flowing. Not interested in food and drink, she lay on her stretcher in a state of abject misery. One of the French nurses who had travelled with her glanced across at the child, Laura intercepting quickly, 'Is there anything she wants? Perhaps *you* might know, Nurse?'

The young woman scrutinised the small girl, then hurriedly searched beneath her covers, shaking her head, and with a tired smile said, '*Mais oui, mon chèr enfant*, I will come back.'

She was in seconds, carrying a soft, battered old toy duck. 'There, *ma chérie*, that is better, *non*?' She kissed the child, who was already showing signs of the tiniest glimmer of a smile in the sad, damp eyes as she hugged the poor thing to her, minus most of its downy fur.

'Thank you.' Laura smiled at the girl. 'You must be feeling very sad having to part with the children.'

'Yes, I do not wish to leave, but they will be 'appier in your 'ospital.' The nurse whispered a quick, '*Excusez-moi*,' and darted over to another of her charges.

Simultaneously Laura noticed that the doctor who had seemed so irate was now nursing a dark-haired baby in his arms. He looked thoroughly at odds with the child, particularly now that it had resumed crying, and the subconscious thought went through her mind that perhaps she should relieve the poor man of the child, who was now nuzzling its sleepy head into his shoulder. She hurried over to him, and he gave her an almost haughty, autocratic glance as she said briskly, 'Won't you let me take the child from you? He seems very tired.'

The man's dark eyes met hers briefly with an expression she could only describe as desperation, as if everything he had been through was revealed at that moment for all the world to see. He shook his head with a sad smile. 'No, I. . . I. . .' His words were slurred with a deadly fatigue. 'He is used to me, but thank you.' The voice was clipped, weary now, as if all his energy had been expended on the final efforts for his patients.

'Yes, of course.' Laura felt embarrassed, feeling as if she had intruded upon some personal tragedy that had surfaced briefly. Putting the thoughts from her, she was rather relieved to see that the reception hall was gradually clearing; at least most of the children had been taken care of.

In the large linen cupboard alongside the six casualty

cubicles she collected fresh face-cloths and small towels to replace those that had been rapidly used up, and on returning to Reception saw Gemma, who appeared somewhat agitated. She was helping one of the ambulance crew remove a sad bundle of possessions, which belonged to the newcomers, on to a trolley, and gave a rather desperate grin.

'I suppose these poor little kids will stop crying somewhere along the line tonight.'

'Let's hope so.' Laura fished in her pocket. 'Look, Miss Menzies told me to give you these three labels for your ward. I think the patients are ready to go now—two teenagers and one toddler. She also said that all we want is to get them packed into bed; who goes where and needs what will be sorted out later after tests and things. She's on the phone in her office at the moment.'

'OK, I'll get upstairs to Primrose now, then. First, though, I must go and tell another of the ambulance crew that we're ready for him to give me a hand, seeing that we're not overflowing with staff.'

'Make sure you choose a good-looking one!'

'You can count on it!' Gemma grinned.

'Must go; there's a doctor over there who needs a helping hand.' As she went towards the man, he still cradled the baby in his arms as if reluctant to let the child go, yet he looked terribly drawn, with a grey look which was beginning to worry her.

Poor guy, she thought, he appears to need treatment as much as the patients. Even as the thought struck her, he glanced up, as if to speak to her, taking a step forward. . .but before Laura could reach him he turned extremely pale, swayed, and thrust the baby out in front of him, trying to speak again unsuccessfully, as instinctively she rushed forward to catch the child safely in her arms before the man collapsed, keeling over and falling unconscious to the floor.

It happened so quickly that at first hardly anyone noticed, except Miss Menzies, who had just emerged from her office.

'It's OK, Staff, you look after the baby,' she said, taking in the situation. She glanced across reception. 'Dr Hudson, over here, please,' she called sharply. 'It's one of the visiting doctors. By the way he looks I think the journey's knocked him out.'

The man's travelling colleague and Tim Hudson moved quickly to where the doctor had fallen. While placing him in the recovery position and clearing his airways, Tim Hudson, kneeling over the man, exploded, 'My God, his chest's covered in blood! Trolley, Nurse, please; we'll get him into a cubicle. We need oxygen, a dextrose-saline drip, blood to be sent for cross-matching, and the mobile X-ray unit. No. 1 theatre to be available. Put out a call for Mr Lomax, please. Emergency. I think he's on one of the wards with the children.'

Laura could overhear all of this while she asked the visiting nurse if she knew what she could get for the child, who now seemed to be quietening down. Smilingly, she took the baby, who decided to suck two of his fingers and watch what was going on, forgetting to cry.

'You per'aps 'ave some warm milk, please, yes?' the girl asked, but glancing anxiously towards the cubicle where the doctor had now been wheeled away from view. She murmured absently, ''E 'as worked too 'ard. Dr Peter should not have come with us today.'

Laura nodded sympathetically, not quite knowing what to say. 'I'll just go and get the milk, and then maybe we can find out what's wrong with the doctor.'

Laura heated a large pan of milk, thinking of the other babies in their care, and poured some into a feeding bottle, and when she returned to Reception the young French nurse seemed very grateful. She was cuddling the child up to her, and explained quietly, ''Is mother died when 'e was born. But 'e is such a dear, good little boy.'

Laura gave a small sigh, shaking her head. 'Poor little soul. But maybe one day he will be happy again, perhaps over here in our country.'

The French girl shrugged. 'Whatever will be, will be.'

'Do you know his name?'

'André. I do not know more.'

Laura nodded, leaving the girl and heading for the cubicle. The man was just being taken upstairs to Theatre, face ashen. Dr Hudson was conversing with Miss Menzies in low tones. The two visiting nurses had taken little André to see him comfortably settled in his cot before saying goodbye to him. The ambulance crew were having tea in the servery before the long journey back to Inverness, where transport would no doubt be available to get the other medics to the airport and return that night.

Certainly the man who collapsed would not be going. Laura only remembered the nurse calling him Peter. She walked over to the second escort doctor, who was now staring into space. She sat beside him.

'It's bad luck for your colleague. He has been working very hard, I imagine.'

The man gave an almost derisory laugh. 'War is hard, *mademoiselle*.' His strong face was lined prematurely, Laura suspected. 'Those of us who are left rarely want to relive those stories, but——' he jerked his head towards the recently vacated cubicle '—the scars remain forever.'

Laura felt rather glad when she heard her name being called. The SNO wanted to see her on Hyacinth. She murmured a quick, '*Au revoir,*' to the man who already seemed deep in his own thoughts, and hurried to the lift and up to her ward.

'Ah, there you are, Staff,' Miss Menzies said. 'I'm glad I didn't put any children on your ward; I decided as things happened that Dr Wentworth—or rather Mr, as he's a surgeon as well as a paediatrics man, from his credentials—will be coming on to this ward. It will be fairly quiet for him up here.

'Apparently he suffered a bad chest wound just three days before leaving for the UK. He wasn't fit to travel but insisted and, of course, his sutures had no time to heal in his debilitated state; hence the bleeding and subsequent collapse. We have him in Theatre at the moment to get the job redone, so we have to look after him. Now I must ring Paris.'

She made to leave, then turned, saying, 'By the way, Sister Ann Weekes will be in tomorrow after her day off; she's in charge of Primrose and Hyacinth. I think you'll like her.'

That evening Laura rang home. She had been putting it off, knowing how things were between her parents. Her father answered the phone. 'Hi, Dad! Just to say everything's OK here.'

'Thank heaven for that, dear; your mother's been as jumpy as a cat since you left. Do you think you'll settle up there, then?' He lowered his voice slightly. 'I'm glad you rang; she'll be going back to Aunt Naomi's later tonight. Trouble is, with this divorce pending I feel we drove you away. It worries me.'

'Don't let it, Dad. I needed a fresh start anyway, and I'm really glad I made it now. I'll write a long letter when I get time. Just let me speak to Mum, then I'll ring off. Take care of yourself, Dad.'

'I will, love. Here's Mum now.'

'Is that you, Laura?'

'Hi, Mum; sorry I haven't been in touch before, but things seem pretty good up here so far, so you're not to worry.'

Her mother sounded nervy and keyed up. It was impossible to speak to her normally when she was like that, but they exchanged enough conversation for the time being. Laura replaced the phone slowly, her thoughts still with her parents, just wishing there were something she could do to put things right between them. If only it were possible to bring back her young brother. . .

She was so busy with thoughts of home, she hardly noticed Gemma until she almost collided with her. 'Sorry! Are you going down to dinner in a minute?'

'Sure. I think we're the lucky ones, not yet having to go on nights. I heard Miss Menzies say just now she's going to start advertising for part-time people for nightstaff; with eight more admissions all virtually needing a nurse each at times, things are going to go crazy here for a while.'

In the dining-room, where Miss Menzies had indicated that she liked staff to have their evening meal because it was more civilised, with an 'end of day' feeling for them, Gemma and Laura found their seats. Conversation was buzzing around the large oak-panelled room about the latest intake. Mary and a plump, pleasant-faced lady—the housekeeper—were keeping an eye on things.

'It's mushroom or game soup tonight, Nurses; which would you like?' Mary asked.

The meal got underway, the two girls soon talking to other members of staff. 'You haven't any children on Hyacinth, have you, Nurse?' a girl, not in uniform, slim and attractive in a harebell suit, asked.

'No,' Laura smiled, 'they've taken the English doctor there—the one who collapsed. He's back from Theatre now. Miss Menzies thought it would be quieter for him.'

The girl gave a light trill of laughter. 'Let's hope so. I'm Ann Weekes, sister on Hyacinth and Primrose! I'm just back from my day and night off.'

Both Gemma and Laura introduced themselves, and the three of them talked their way through the entire meal, until Ann stood up suddenly. 'Must go; I have to wash my hair. See you both tomorrow, then!'

On duty next morning, Laura couldn't contain a certain curiosity to renew her brief acquaintance with Peter Wentworth. Night Sister was discussing her night report with several of the day staff.

'Now, our new admission, Mr Wentworth. He has a rather nasty bullet wound—clean, though, an in-and-out job. The sutures had to be replaced, as some of you may know. Dr Lomax mentioned using a seaweed dressing that heals as well as treating any infection that might be present. He'll confirm when he does his round. The patient also slept reasonably.'

She turned a page of the report book. 'The twin boys. No problems with them.' She grinned, saying, 'For Laura and Gemma's benefit, we call them Cain and Abel because we can't pronounce their names properly! They had a reasonable night's sleep. They're lying on waterbeds to help the bedsore problem. To us they still look like living skeletons but progress, although slow, is being made. They're on a strict regime of Elemental iron and sulphate dosage for nutritional anaemia. Folic acid orally for seven to fourteen days. Vitamin E and K, as well as protein. It's all on their charts. Dr Lomax is very fussy about it. He seems to think there's something else wrong with them, but as yet they haven't the strength to put up with all the tests, et cetera.'

She sighed. 'It's early days, I suppose, to see signs of real improvement; we've only had them here such a short time. Now we come to Janek. He needed pain-killers in the night. No bleeding of the wound.' She glanced up at Laura. 'His dressing will need changing today, so Ann will take you through that,' she said. 'Knowing him, he'll join in! It's really amazing what that man has absorbed since he arrived.'

The door opened just then and Sister Weekes came in with a bright smile. 'Morning, everyone! I've just collected the post, always hoping there'll be something for our patients, but nothing so far. Usually staff only.'

The night nurse was collecting up her things. 'Well, bye, then; see you tonight!'

'Bye; sleep well!'

Gemma went across to Primrose, Ann and Laura to Hyacinth to say their good mornings to the four males, three smiling and Peter Wentworth, pillows supporting him, sitting up, eyes closed, features immobile.

Ann frowned slightly. 'Doesn't seem too lively, yet he had a good night. I think we'll leave him for a while.'

At breakfast-time, Laura took a tray to Peter Wentworth's bedside. He was awake, more or less. 'Good morning, Mr Wentworth; you had a good night's sleep, it seems.'

Long, dark lashes fluttered open and raven-black brows lifted slightly as he stared at Laura, as if unsure where he was, then a glimmer of recognition appeared and he murmured, 'Thank you, yes.' He struggled to raise himself up a little as she stacked his pillows more comfortably, at the same time full consciousness seemed to strike him when he demanded suddenly, 'The children we brought in last night; are they near by?'

'Yes, in Primrose, just across the corridor there,' she told him, placing the tray on his bed-table. 'I suggest you have some food now; it will do you more good than worrying about your little charges at the moment,' she said kindly.

He gave her a morose stare, as if she were miles removed from the realities of life. 'I can't eat this morning; I'm sorry.'

'Well, I'll leave the tray in case you change your mind,' she said brightly. 'The boiled eggs are very nice and fresh; they come from free-range chickens on the home farm here.'

'Really?' he said lugubriously.

Later, Ann and Laura returned to his bedside, to find the tray still untouched, which did not deter Ann's cheerful greeting. 'Hi, Mr Wentworth! How's the world looking to you this morning?'

'Morning to you both!' The eyes that had appeared so full of pain the night before were now at least alert and obviously wanting to know all that was going on around him. 'My thanks to everyone,' he said quietly, 'I'm very grateful to you. Do you happen to know if anyone's been in touch with Paris?'

'Yes,' Laura said, 'Miss Menzies dealt with it last night.'

'Thank heaven for that.'

Ann took a quick glance at his medical chart. 'Everything seems very satisfactory as well, so just have a good rest. I'm Sister Ann Weekes and this is Staff Nurse Laura Meadows. She's my number two, so to speak, and arrived here a couple of days ago.'

The dark ink-blue eyes met hers; his long, lean jaw sported an early stubble over a well-lived-in suntan. A brief smile hovered about the firm, well-shaped lips. 'Laura Meadows—the one who did a flying leap across the room for the baby yesterday before the ground came up and hit me.'

'Well, that could be a pretty accurate description,

yes,' Laura agreed, feeling herself blush. It was the way the man's eyes had almost twinkled, as if in better times a sense of humour lurked there.

'I'm indebted to you. I think I heard your name mentioned when I was on the way to the operating theatre yesterday.'

Ann stepped in. 'Right, you must conserve your energy now, Mr Wentworth. You'll be seeing Mr Lomax when he does his round this morning; he'll give you all your instructions as to what you must and mustn't do. We all know doctors prefer to be at the bedside instead of in it!' She grinned at Laura, having noticed Janek give Peter Wentworth a friendly wave. 'We'll leave these men to their idle chatter for now, Staff.' To the men she said, 'Don't get up to any mischief, now!'

As they left the ward Ann said thoughtfully, 'That Mr Wentworth has a lot on his mind; I wish I knew what it was. I get the feeling he's not going to be too sociable.'

Primrose ward was very quiet. In a separate side-ward were three men, and one of the younger ones was trying to make some sense of what Dennis was endeavouring to convey to him with some rather elaborate sign language.

'Good old Dennis,' Ann murmured. 'As a charge nurse he's great to work with, although being of equivalent rank, he and I have to try and take our off-duty times separately, so we don't actually get to work together very often.'

'I can see the difficulties,' Laura said, noticing Mr Lomax striding into Hyacinth ward.

Ann had spotted him too. 'Perhaps you'll go round with him, please, Laura. We're not strictly surgical on this side. Actually, there's a possibility of Aids with the three on the side-ward, although it hasn't yet been confirmed. It's so hard when they've been through so much. The young one talking to Dennis is having a cystoscopy in a few days' time. They're all on masses of vitamin intake before a lot can be done. I'm amazed how some of them withstood the journey here.'

As Laura was about to go to Hyacinth, the phone rang and she answered it. An agitated voice asked for Sister Weekes. 'I'll go and get her,' Laura said, and, having done so, joined Mr Lomax, who was at Peter Wentworth's bedside, both men chatting animatedly.

'Morning, Staff! How are you settling in?'

'Great, thanks.'

Mr Lomax was not a proud man; he had already drawn the curtains around Peter's bed, not in the least concerned with protocol. Laura was coming to recognise this practical attitude as typically Scottish.

Ann appeared at the doors. 'Laura, can I have a word, please?' Her face was pale and worried. 'Look, I've got to go; Tony, my husband, has had some kind of accident. That was my mother on the phone. Will you carry on with the dressing. I must go and see Miss Menzies now.'

Laura wheeled the laid-up dressings trolley that Pearl had prepared earlier into the ward, her thoughts and her sympathy with Ann. She just hoped it was not too serious. Mr Lomax was ready to examine the wound; wearing mask and gloves, Laura turned back the patient's bedclothes to reveal the newly sutured area on Peter Wentworth's broad, muscular chest. Mr Lomax straightened up, giving a sigh of satisfaction.

'So far, so good, Peter! I'm going to get Staff to apply a seaweed dressing we use here called Kaltostat.' He turned to Laura. 'When you do it, Staff, make sure the dressing is thoroughly soaked with the stuff. That's all!' He wagged a finger at his colleague. 'A good rest now, my boy, for two or three days, anyway!'

Laura returned to the drugs cupboard to collect the bottle of Kaltostat, just hoping there would be one to hand. To her relief there was. There were still gaps in their supplies which needed to be filled. Apart from the obvious necessities, Miss Menzies had hinted, with her native caution, that with lesser used treatments it was the only way to prevent wastage.

Back on the ward, Mr Lomax was examining the twins, Pearl attending him. Laura stepped inside Peter Wentworth's drawn bed-curtains where he was lying in a semi-supine position, waiting patiently to have his wound dressed.

She was very much aware of his interest as he watched her. 'Sorry to keep you, Mr Wentworth, but we're all still feeling our way around here, as it were. I'm sure you know by now that the Lodge has only recently been opened as a charity hospital.'

'A very good one, too, as far as I can see.'

She busied herself with spreading a small white waterproof sheet to protect the bedlinen, embarrassingly conscious of the fine texture of his skin and the width of his shoulders. Quickly she said with a grin, 'So glad you approve.' Which was a trite answer she should have known better than to make to a superior, and she knew that a certain kind of nervousness was to blame.

'How long have you been here? You did tell me, I think, but I've forgotten—no, wait, I haven't forgotten; I think it was Sister who mentioned it a short while ago. Two days, is that right?'

She chuckled at his rather too serious manner as he watched her place sterile cloths on the perimeter of his wound. 'Yes, I just beat you to it!'

'Of course! Well, you seem to have settled in very well.' His expression was genuinely sincere as she turned to draw the trolley towards her, pouring the

Kaltostat into a kidney dish and soaking the new dressing thoroughly.

'I just happened to be here at the right time,' she said casually, removing the sterile cloths from his chest. 'This will be cold,' she warned, then covered the sutured area well across his torso. 'Just lean further forward towards me, please.' She bound the area with a broad crêpe bandage, then urged him back again on to the pillows.

His eyes had been upon her throughout the whole procedure, and, as so often, she cursed her fair complexion that made her appear to blush too easily, which on this occasion had been prompted by his murmured, 'Thank you, Staff, that feels very comfortable.' And there was a slight intonation in the deep voice that made her certain that it was not all he'd intended to say.

Probably her imagination, she thought as she returned the trolley back to the sluice and cleared it. Nevertheless, there was no doubt he seemed to be improving and was now showing signs of becoming a little more gregarious. She just hoped it would last.

Later, she was checking the special morning drinks and gruels for some of the patients, when Pearl came in. 'Have you seen Ann, Laura?'

'No, not in the last half-hour. Come to think of it, I haven't seen her since she had a phone call earlier; she thought Tony had had an accident of some kind.'

'Oh, poor old Ann,' Pearl murmured. 'OK, then; it's just that I was going down to talk to Miss Menzies. I had an appointment to discuss my holiday period for later this year.'

'You go, Pearl. As far as I know Dennis has switched back to days now that Gemma and I are here.'

'Great. I'll be back as soon as I can.'

Laura took the drinks round with a trainee nurse

from Primrose; she was a nice girl but rather shy and, because of it, asked Laura if she would mind taking the newly admitted doctor's drink to him. 'OK, but he doesn't bite, you know!' Laura said.

Peter Wentworth appeared to be sleeping, his curtains now drawn back, morning sunlight striking across his face, revealing a small network of tired lines around his eyes. She still wondered about him; there were so many questions she'd like to ask, but of course couldn't possibly. It was simply something she felt towards him that made her want to. . .well, just talk to him. . .

His eyes opened suddenly, and again she felt embarrassed as, with a smile, she placed the hot chocolate drink on his beside locker. 'Sorry if I disturbed you.'

He gave a wry grin. 'Not a bit. In fact I'd quite like you to sit down and talk to me for the next two hours about anything and everything. I feel as if I've been away from home forever.'

'And how long is it?'

'Four years in all. Managed to get home just once or twice, although one of those occasions was mostly business—a short lecture series to some medical students at Edinburgh.'

She signalled to the trainee to give her a hand. 'You need to be sitting up higher than you are,' Laura told him. 'Would you like a bed-rest or more pillows?'

'Pillows, please, Staff,' he answered, with a curve of his lips, as if being a patient was a source of some amusement to him.

'Nurse, fetch three more pillows from the airing cupboard, will you, please?'

When the girl returned, Laura put the pillows in place and together they each took an arm and hoisted him further up the bed. He winced but said nothing. Laura retained a businesslike approach and yet at the same time was very conscious of the half-smile still hovering upon this man's features, his gaze assessing her. 'There we are, then,' she said, the task completed. 'OK, Nurse, thanks. Will you give Janek his drink now? She passed Peter his chocolate. 'Enjoy it, then you can go back to sleep!'

'So,' he mocked unexpectedly, 'just as I'm made utterly contented, you desert me!'

She raised laughing eyes to the ceiling. 'Who was it said that doctors make the most terrible patients?' she called over her shoulder, feeling a ridiculous sense of achievement at Peter Wentworth's sudden note of cheerfulness.

When she returned to her office on hearing the telephone ring, she said to the young girl, 'I'll take it, Nurse. See that the twins get their warm milk in feeding cups; you'll have to help them.' She lifted the receiver. 'Staff Nurse Meadows.'

'Miss Menzies here, Laura. I'm afraid poor Ann Weekes has had very bad news. Tony has been involved in a road accident; it appears to be much worse than they'd at first thought. He was apparently coaxing some sheep across the road—a mere country lane comparatively speaking—to the other side for lambing, when an idiot driver came hurtling round the corner scattering the sheep, killing some as well as the sheepdog. Ann's husband was badly injured, the tragedy being that he wasn't found for some half-hour after it happened.'

'Oh, my goodness, how dreadful,' Laura murmured, deeply shocked. 'Where have they taken Tony?'

'First to the local cottage hospital at Dornoch, but things were so bad he's now on his way to Inverness. Ann's with him, of course, which brings me to the situation here. Will you take over in her place until we know more, Laura? With help from Dennis and Gemma, do you think you can manage?'

'I'm sure of it, Miss Menzies,' she said quickly, feeling a small glow of pride to have been asked. 'I'll help in any way I can until Ann comes back.'

'Good girl. Don't forget to come and see me if you have any problems. I'll let everyone know the minute we hear something positive about Tony. Oh, and by the way, I've been so taken up with this problem I haven't had a chance to get up to the wards this morning. How is Mr Wentworth?'

'Satisfactory, I would say. Not so low-spirited as when he first arrived.'

'Good. He's probably less worried about those children now. I hear he's had a fearful time in the fighting zones; can't wonder at him being subdued, to say the least.'

Once she was back on the ward Miss Menzies' words hung about in Laura's mind, especially when later she took the lunchtime menu in to him. 'How would you like baked turbot and green vegetables, followed by raspberry fool, Mr Wentworth?' she asked brightly, hoping to rekindle his rising spirits a little more. But she was to be disappointed.

A frown had settled upon his brow as he said absently, 'Anything, thanks, Staff.'

'Hey, come on, Mr Wentworth! From what I gather you have to make up for lost time—eating-wise, I mean,' she encouraged with a smile.

The words faded on her lips when she saw the black expression now confronting her. 'There are far more important things in life, Staff—as far as I'm concerned, anyway. I've realised recently how little one can exist on. So I repeat, I'm not that interested.'

'I see,' she said curtly, trying hard to make allowances for his sudden change of mood.

'I'm not so sure that you do, Staff,' he answered

cryptically, eyes locking with hers as if she knew very little at all. 'How is it possible?'

The question was derisive, his sardonic tone getting to her. How the hell did he know what she had done or not done, as the case may be? Anger surged within her as thoughts of her young brother, whom she had so recently lost, came into her mind.

The year before, while still a medical student during vacation, he had cajoled her to go along with him on a voluntary supply trip by heavy-duty lorry to Bosnia. Things they had seen out there had made him determined to return to work on the medical teams once he was qualified—just a few months away. He had talked of nothing else on the long, cold, winter journey home; a few weeks later he had been killed.

A tremor shook her voice as she raised her chin. 'There cannot be too many of us, Mr Wentworth, who have not been deeply moved by media reports and pictures,' she said tersely, tweaking his bedcover straight as an excuse to conceal the tell-tale quiver of her chin.

For a moment he stared at her, then answered brusqely, 'Admittedly, such duties cannot fall to all of us. . .' Her violet gaze mesmerised him briefly, the thought occurring that he had angered her in some way—her cheeks were crimson, eyes a smouldering brilliance conveying a sensitivity which seemed to pierce his heart.

Laura took a deep breath to calm herself and responded simply, 'Help is needed the world over, unfortunately, Mr Wentworth.' She was annoyed now that she had allowed this man's comment to get under her skin; she really must remain composed. She managed a smile and deliberately perked up. 'Anyhow,' she said lightly, 'I still thoroughly recommend the turbot!'

Unexpectedly he gave her a gentle smile, as if they had both recognised an unspoken truce between them.

'Right! Turbot it shall be! And how are the children this morning?'

CHAPTER THREE

AT LUNCHTIME, in the servery for staff, there was a subdued air about the place in deference to Ann Weekes' husband and the shock his accident had caused. He was apparently such a jovial, happy man, and no one could imagine Ann without him, they were such a devoted couple.

Gemma toyed with her fish pie. 'I know you and I don't actually know Tony, Laura, but why is it that such nice, happy people so often get the rotten luck? It doesn't make sense, does it?'

'Heaven knows,' Laura said absently, the shock once again bringing back the terrible trauma of her brother's accident. For the second time that day she began to realise fully the awful effect it must have had upon her parents. She remembered her father buying the motorbike for her brother's twenty-first birthday to get about while he was at university, and the fuss her mother had made.

When the worst had happened Laura had thought only of the loss that she herself had suffered. Now she could see beyond that point and it was no longer hard to realise why her parents were at such cross-purposes with each other. She at least had been resident at her hospital in Colchester, and had had a break from the terrible sense of loss and emptiness when she'd been there, but for them there could be no let-up.

Gemma was speaking to her. 'Don't you think so, Laura?'

'Sorry, I didn't get that.'

'I was saying maybe poor old Ann will be giving up

her job if Tony is unable to carry on with the farm.'

'Maybe. Which reminds me, I've just come back from seeing Miss Menzies; she wants me to step into Ann's shoes temporarily until we see what happens. I imagine she'll be telling you, anyway.'

Laura thought she saw a fleeting expression of. . . jealousy?. . .in Gemma's eyes. No. It couldn't be. The arrangement was purely temporary, wasn't it? 'How is little André, by the way?' she said quickly. 'I haven't had time to pop over to see him today.'

'He's great really. I think a lot of love will get him through.'

'Let's hope you're right. Looking at him, I'd say malnutrition is the only thing he seems to be suffering from at present, thank goodness.'

The servery was rapidly emptying. Joan Barnard came in, not joining the other doctors but sitting on her own at a table in the window. Gemma glanced at Laura, raising an eyebrow. 'I wonder what it is with that woman? She seems determined to isolate herself, doesn't she?'

Laura stood up. 'Difficult to know, but we all have our troubles. See you after my two hours off this afternoon, then I must rearrange our duty hours again with this new development. Good job ours is a charity concern, eh?'

She was glad to get back to her room for the short break. Deep in thought, she made herself a cup of peppermint tea to try and stave off a slight headache that was threatening. It had to be because of the talk she'd had with Peter Wentworth. She ought not to have allowed him to disturb her peace of mind, and realised now just how sensitive she still was about her brother's death.

On the two-seater settee in her comfortable bedroom, she curled her feet up beneath her to avoid lying on the bed and falling into a deep sleep. Even so, she was peeved to find that her thoughts kept returning to Peter Wentworth. She certainly had no feelings of attraction for him in the real sense after so recently being free of Keith. It was just that this man, who had entered her life so unexpectedly, at once irritated and intrigued her, and she supposed that in a way it was this combination, as well as his compassion—not without a certain charm—that led her to these conclusions.

Nevertheless, still very much aware of his mood swings, she vowed to try and tolerate them. Besides, it shouldn't be too long before he was up and about.

On returning to her office later she telephoned the duty changes to Miss Menzies, and then went across to Primrose to see the new patients admitted since the three men had been moved to a side-ward. They now had two teenagers, twelve and sixteen respectively, two babies and one toddler, André the youngest. All were undernourished, all pathetically quiet and, as far as the babies were concerned, remaining as still as when they had first been placed in their cots, large eyes in wasted faces just staring at the comings and goings in front of them.

Laura peeped into André's cot. His big eyes had more expression in them, and she was quite sure a fleeting glance of recognition passed between them. At least, that was what she liked to think it was. She ran a hand over his smooth cheek. 'Hi, darling!' she murmured. 'Are you going to give me a little smile, then?' After more baby talk she was sure his tiny feet began to pump weakly up and down. She leaned over and dropped a kiss on his forehead. 'You gorgeous creature——'

'You can say that to me any time!' a male voice said behind her. It was Dennis, clutching André's bottle of warm milk laced with vitamins, wrapped in a snow-white towelling cloth.

'Hi, Dennis! Has Miss Menzies told you that I'm now your temporary counterpart?'

'Oh, yes, and I have to keep an eye on you, she said, like cuddling this baby and you giving him his milk instead of me!'

Still laughing, Laura went back to her office on Hyacinth. Pearl was there, setting out the TPR trolley and needing the drug-cupboard keys. 'Pearl, did you get your holidays sorted out OK?'

'Yes, thanks, Staff. I haven't thought about it too much since hearing of Ann's troubles.'

'I know, terrible, isn't it?'

'I hear you've taken her job over for a while. Good thing you and Gemma turned up when you did,' she said, moving the trolley out and leaving it in a locked room.

'Have you checked that there's no further bleeding on Janek's leg stump? It started again yesterday, but up until this morning it was OK.'

'I'll go and check again now.'

'Right. Then I'll get the clean bedlinen organised. Once we've done beds and sore-prevention it'll be nearly dinnertime.'

It must have been two hours or so later that, to Laura's great surprise, she heard the sound of talking and laughter coming from the ward. Janek was conversing animatedly with Cain and Abel in their own language, and Peter Wentworth, of all people, was joining in! Every now and again great gusts of laughter emerged from them all.

They stopped when she appeared. 'Oh, please, do carry on! It's wonderful to hear you all talking together for once!' She looked across at Peter Wentworth; his face was less drawn, and wreathed in smiles. 'My goodness, this is something we've all longed for—that we might suddenly acquire a linguist in our midst! I mean, look!' She threw her arm out to the three happy faces. 'It's going to make a fantastic difference that they'll be able to communicate.'

He nodded, with a small grin of pleasure, saying chirpily, 'Oh, it's just a lucky knack I have for languages. And it could most certainly be a step in the right direction.'

'And the specific language you were speaking just now?' she asked, trying to keep a look of admiration from her eyes.

'Serbo-Croat. Quite a lot of people from Eastern Europe use it as a second language, much as the rest of the world does English.'

Laura smiled happily. 'Well, I think we'll have to set up the Hyacinth and Primrose Language Academy here, you know! There's enough people in the Lodge for us to need the exchange and learning of half a dozen different tongues!'

Peter Wentworth nodded approvingly. 'I'm beginning to think that might have been one of the Duke's original ideas when he first decided to free the Lodge. What better reason to be able to speak to each other and create global peace instead of war?'

'My sentiments also!' Laura trilled happily, almost unable to believe, as she went off to write her report, that things had taken such a turn for the better.

Despite the mundanities of general routine, she had quite a lot on her mind; notwithstanding, each time she walked into the ward she was conscious of Peter Wentworth's presence. His long, angular figure seemed totally out of place in the comparatively narrow bed, and yet how much more animated he was beginning to look since he had first arrived. She couldn't decide whether she was intrigued by him still; she had noticed a very faint touch of superiority emerging. To be wary of him was the main thing, she instructed herself firmly.

However, next day, while attending to his dressing, she relented a fraction. He was even more lively, as if his assistance with their language problems had given him a genuine uplift, away from some of his more morose conversations. When he leant forward to request that his bandage be secured, he murmured in her ear, 'Delighted, Staff. . .!' He was smiling. 'I shall have to make certain Mr Lomax instructs that my dressing be done each day. . .' The dark eyes were looking up into hers as he settled back upon the pillows.

And despite the rose colour that suffused her cheeks she said with a grin, 'And I can tell you, Mr Wentworth, that Pearl's hands are a whole lot colder than mine when she likes!'

'Now don't spoil my day, Staff; you've done splendidly so far.'

She averted her face as she repacked the trolley. 'Something tells me that flattery has more often than not been quite advantageous in your lifetime!' she said boldly.

'When you have time, I'll tell you the whole unexpurgated version!'

'Ha Ha! "When" being the operative word!' She drew back his curtains. 'There we are, then! That, my good doctor, is you finished!' she said flippantly, marvelling that she was addressing him this way.

'Don't sound so pleased—there's always tomorrow, you know!'

Two days after that decidedly brighter episode, Peter Wentworth had confirmation from Mr Lomax that his wound was healing well. Laura and Pearl were doing their best to prevent him from over-exertion;

nevertheless, that afternoon he was happily esconced
in a wheelchair in the kitchen doorway, talking to the
two girls as they prepared special teas for the wards.
Peter, wearing a wine-red silk dressing-gown that had
been loaned him, as he had no luggage at all, was in
full flood about teaching foreign patients English. His
face was intent, alive with enthusiasm.

'I know some of them are too young, but I'll think
of something later for them. If I can get the teenagers
and the older ones to join in, word will soon get round,
and it can only be for the good of all. Do you think
we can get something going, Laura?'

More recently he had insisted upon first names
between them all, unless formality forbade it. Everyone agreed with this, for since his language ability had
become known he was something of a hero.

Laura was busily checking the non-spill beakers for
the toddler, and drinking bottles for the babies. 'Well,
as we said before, it's a great idea. I'm sure Miss
Menzies would approve. But see how things go on our
two wards here first. The children, for instance, are
getting used to you now. I mean, even young André
manages to give you a little gurgle when you go and
say good morning to him!'

'He does, doesn't he? He'll probably be one of my
first infant prodigies!'

When he had gone, Pearl gave a grin. 'He's really
taken to that baby, hasn't he?'

'Yes, although I think it's mainly because he obviously set himself to care for the child since they first
arrived, and don't forget André's mother died giving
birth to him. His father's dead, I suppose. No one's
ever mentioned it; we've just assumed he's an orphan.
Peter's certainly got a soft spot for children.'

'Is he married himself?' Pearl asked.

Laura looked at the tall girl. 'Pearl! Ask me something easy! We don't know much about any of them yet.'

Pearl grinned. 'Well, I'll tell you one thing—a good-looking guy like him must have been too busy playing the field to have time for marriage!'

'You never know.' Laura spread a freshly laundered tea-towel over the clean teacups and beakers. 'I wonder if the patients ever have thoughts about us? Though I'm not very interesting for a start, anyway!'

'Neither am I. But I do have a lazy good-for-nothing husband who wants to be an actor just because he did a TV commercial in sports gear——' She stopped suddenly and sighed, saying, 'But boy, that man of mine has *some* muscles.'

'Come on, Pearl, you know you think he's wonderful. He'll probably become a rich film star one day and then you'll leave us.'

Pearl gave a delightful giggle. 'Don't worry about that—unless they make me a star too. . . Dreams. . . dreams. . .!'

That evening, just after Pearl and the trainee had gone off duty, and before the night nurse came on, Laura went to talk to Janek, as far as was possible—anything really important had to be said through Peter—but Janek was interested in other things. At that moment he was sitting up gazing at a photograph. When he saw Laura he thrust it forward for her to look at. A very pretty woman, possibly in her mid-thirties, smiled back at her, a cloud of black curly hair to her shoulders, and she was wearing a white, rather provocative off-the-shoulder blouse edged with magnificent lace, and large gold gypsy earrings.

Laura nodded and widened her eyes with approval. 'She is beautiful, Janek, very beautiful.'

'Yes. . . *Ja*. . . *Oui*. . .' he agreed, in whichever language seemed to strike him.

'Your wife?'

Janek threw back his head with laughter, shaking his head from side to side as if that was the last thing in the world he wanted. He was still chuckling to himself when Laura did the rest of the round, finishing with Peter. He was comfortably established in bed by now, and, when she arrived, put aside his *Times*.

'Laura,' he said quietly, 'I've arranged to have a medical next week. I want to get back to work.'

She frowned. 'You mean to Bosnia or somewhere?' She couldn't quite believe what he was saying. For some crazy reason she had expected him to be with them for ages yet, what with the talk of him setting up language classes and advising on some of the children's backgrounds he might be aware of.

'It could be Bosnia, or anywhere I'm needed.' His eyes met hers and it was as if she could not wrench them away. 'You don't approve?'

She pulled herself together. 'Well, in my opinion it may be a little too soon, but you will no doubt discuss it with Mr Lomax.'

'As a matter of fact I already have, and he says provided I pass a thorough medical test with the doctors here there's no reason why I couldn't apply to return to Europe, at least.'

'I see. Well——' she gave a short laugh '—just make the most of all the pampering you're getting now, then!'

Later, Gemma and Laura sat in her room in their dressing-gowns, sharing a bottle of wine that someone had given Dennis, and he'd passed on because he didn't drink. Gemma stared into the imitation log fire that was necessary, even though spring was well underway. 'Good of old Dennis, wasn't it? Do you think he's. . .

you know. . .gay?' she said suddenly. 'He's a bit flirty, but it's difficult to know, isn't it?'

'Whatever he is, he's jolly nice, I think.'

'Yeah, me too. We'll have to try and find him a girlfriend and see what happens!'

'You turning into an agony aunt or something?'

'Not me; I've too many love tangles of my own to sort out.'

'Have you heard any more from Ken since that phone call?'

'No, he's sulking, I bet. Men!' Gemma said.

'Talking of which, did you know that Peter Wentworth's applying for a medical so that he can go back to his job with the Red Cross and aid workers?'

'No, I didn't. I'd rather had the feeling he was going to stay in this country now. He has parents here in Edinburgh, according to Doc Hudson. He said they were in the middle of a sea cruise when Peter was brought in, and he had a message sent saying he was fine and there was nothing to rush home for.'

'Cool customer. Good job they didn't see him when he first arrived, then.'

'Too true.'

Laura yawned, pushing her arms high above her head. 'I think I'll turn in now; must be the wine. I'm off in the morning and I intend borrowing a bike to cycle into the village. If you want anything let me know.'

'OK. Thanks.' Gemma got up and opened the door. 'God, I can hear the phone ringing. If it's Ken I'll brain him, phoning at this time of night!'

Next morning it was cold, but the sun shone and Laura was quite looking forward to her first trip out beyond the Lodge. She was dressed for warmth: jeans, thick

navy guernsey, trainers and blue padded anorak. She
had tied her hair back, checked that she had her list
in her pocket, and that was it. All she needed now
was a bicycle.

She had been directed by Dennis to a lovely old
barn where several cycles stood in a rack. They all
looked in good condition, and she selected one, gave
the tyres an extra pump, and was ready. It was breezy
and as an afterthought she wrapped a long woollen
scarf around her neck. As she was tying it she saw a
man walk from the front entrance of the Lodge. He
was tall, dressed in an anorak and casual trousers, good
leather shoes, and standing as if sniffing the air. She
was so busy looking at him that as she mounted the
bike she wobbled rather dangerously, and a baker's
van suddenly appeared, unpleasantly close. It swerved
away from her and turned into the drive at the side
of the house.

It gave her such a fright, she wobbled again and
went sprawling down on to the gravel, the bike on
top of her.

'I can't let you out of my sight for five minutes, can
I? Are you OK?'

It was Peter Wentworth helping her up, brushing
her down, while she felt an absolute idiot. 'I'm fine,
thanks—really. It was the baker's van that gave me a
surprise,' she said limply, realising a strong arm was
still supporting her.

'Well, we do have traffic up here—occasionally,' he
grinned. 'More importantly, are you going to be safe
with that thing?'

'Nothing to it,' she smiled, then tried to change the
subject, feeling his arm move from her. 'I hope you've
had permission to come outside like this?'

'From the highest authorities! How do you like the
outfit?'

'Very fetching. I've only ever seen you in a half a pair of pyjamas so far!'

'That could be construed as a slanderous statement!'

'Well, it could be, but it's true. We can't count the night you arrived. I wouldn't remember what you wore then anyway.'

'I hardly remember myself. Anyhow, these are borrowed plumes but it won't be long before I go and fit myself out with one or two items of my own gear.' He gave her a long look, that teasing smile appearing about his lips. 'You look pretty good yourself this morning.'

'When in Rome. . .and all that!'

'Yes, I imagine it's all heathery tweeds and woollen unmentionables at this time of year!'

'More or less. It's beautiful, though, I just love it. Now, is there anything I can get you in the village—a pair of socks, a suit, a deerstalker hat?'

'No, thanks,' he chuckled. 'Just be careful on that thing and get back in one piece.'

'It's not a thing, it's a bike!' She gave him a small grin. 'I can't get started when someone's watching me!'

'I won't look, but I'll hold the bike steady while you climb on if you like!'

'No, thanks—my father used to do that when I was five.' Laura laughed, sure that she had not been on one of these contraptions since then. It was positively Edwardian. She got away, despite the front wheel being somewhat erratic, calling over her shoulder, 'Thanks for your help. 'Bye!'

It was easy to follow the signs to the village of Brora; there was nowhere else to go. When she arrived, having pushed against a headwind, her legs felt as if she had done ten miles rather than five.

The little village itself was picturesque in the morning sunshine. Its main attraction, as far as the male

ancients were concerned, was leaning over the parapet
of a mellow brick road bridge that spanned a lively
river, its banks as yet touched only by a faint veil of
spring green. Clear water gushed joyfully over flat
round boulders on its way to the sea, by all accounts
just minutes away.

There were several hotels, a small car park, and a
collection of small useful shops which Laura felt could
at least supply what she had on her list. She was right,
and when she had finished she bought a Coke at a
sweet shop and set off again, the ride back, with the
wind behind her, quite exhilarating.

When she reached the loch she slowed down a little,
the water as blue as some of the postcards of it which
she'd seen in a souvenir shop. She could hear on the
soft air the first stirrings of the spring birdsong. Two
herons appeared at a safe distance across the loch,
intent on nesting, a wood pigeon cooed, and a chiff-
chaff fluttered across her handlebars as she continued
leisurely along the path to the Lodge. She would have
so loved to bring some of the sick children out here,
to see them fit and well enough to absorb the sights and
scenes their young senses had not enjoyed probably for
months on end—if at all.

Back on duty that afternoon, she found Peter
Wentworth sitting in an armchair alongside his bed,
reading. When she entered the ward with the tea, he
smiled, immediately asking about the village trip.

'Super!' she smiled, surprised—but not quite knowing why—to see the title of his book; *An Anthology
of British Composers*. 'It's a lovely little place,' she
said, describing it. 'There's even a tiny harbour, and,
tucked nicely out of sight, an immaculate railway
station with a direct main line to London!'

'Who could ask for more?' he grinned as he put his

book aside, compelled to watch the sparkling animation on her face. 'The bike didn't let you down?'

'No, neither did I get a puncture! How are you feeling after venturing out into the great wide world?'

'I could get used to it! In fact Mr Lomax came up to tell me this afternoon I had passed their medical, and, according to my wishes, arranged for me to attend a board to confirm I'm considered fit enough to return to Europe for work.'

'When will this be?'

'Tuesday of next week.'

'If they pass you, how long before you return to work?'

'A week maybe.' He looked drawn suddenly, as if thinking of it tired him. He stood up, giving her a half-smile that tilted his mouth so attractively. 'I think I'll go and see how André is; he was sleeping when I went in this morning.'

She watched him walk away, as if deep in thought.

She tidied Janek's empty bed, still thinking of Peter's possible departure, then switched her mind to Janek. He had been taken that day to Inverness to be measured for an artificial leg. She missed his smiling face, and hoped his leg stump formed to a cone with a smooth surface, and was adequate in its preparation for the subsequent fitting of the limb. Whatever happened, he was a man of forceful character and courage, and she felt sure he would adapt in the way he had to.

She looked at the twins; neither had been too well in the last few days. They were awaiting results of tests, as it seemed that both might have contracted tuberculosis and would need to be moved from the Lodge to Inverness or Wick. She found them sleeping deeply, and took the feeding cups back to the kitchen, then prepared the drugs trolley for the evening. Just then a voice broke into her thoughts. . .

'You have pretty ankles, do you know that?'

She swung round. Peter Wentworth was smiling at her. 'Now I really do know you're feeling recovered!' she teased, aware of the wretched blush stealing across her cheeks.

'No, I mean it. I believe in giving credit where it's due!'

'Well, thank you. I shall think of that when you're in far-flung places and be glad!'

'Glad that I'm in far-flung places?'

'No, idiot, that perhaps my ankles weren't quite as bad as I thought!'

'I think——' He stopped suddenly, a far-away expression on his face. 'It doesn't matter.'

She said quickly, 'How did you find André?'

'He was awake and hung on to my finger, would you believe? He's quite a knowing little chap. Physically speaking, one great relief is that so far we've spotted nothing that's indicative of him needing anything more than the loving care and good food he's getting.'

'Yes, he's certainly one of the lucky ones—at the moment, anyway. I hope things won't be difficult for him later. You've no idea where his father is?'

'No idea,' he said rather absently, then, 'Laura, should you see Miss Menzies some time before you go off duty tonight, would you ask if I could see her tomorrow morning, provided she's not too busy?'

'Sure.' She gave him a stern look, although her eyes were soft. 'I suggest you get back into bed now. Only then will I bring you a second cup of tea.'

'You're a hard woman, Laura Meadows!'

'Soft inside though, Mr Wentworth!' she laughed as she drew his curtains, then went along to the office to cope with some admin.

The next seven days went by very quickly at the Lodge, with the continued absence of Ann, whose husband was still in Intensive Care, leaving her to organise a temporary farm manager. She was taking leave until Tony's injuries, which included a ruptured spleen and fractured ribs, gave no further cause for alarm.

Laura had just taken some flowers into the ward, given by a local benefactor, when Mr Lomax rang. 'Morning, Laura. About the twins' tests; it's as we thought, I'm afraid. They must have had primary TB in their infanthood. The lymph glands healed, but left only some immunity. Now, of course, the disease has become more active, helped along by poor nourishment and debilitation. I need to get them to Inverness. I've told Miss Menzies; she'll be in touch.'

'Right, thanks, Mr Lomax.'

'By the way, I presume Peter is out on one of his keep-fit walks?'

'He is, as a matter of fact.'

'Right. I'll be up to see him after lunch.'

Laura replaced the receiver slowly. She was sad about the twins; they were so quiet and passive in their appreciative attitude for all that was done for them. She so hoped the disease would be cured for good and all now, once they'd received the right treatment.

She took Janek and Cain and Abel their drinks, having a cheery word with them all, telling the twins they were being moved and doing her best to make it sound like a big opportunity for them. Peter would give them the true facts later, in their own language. Then the phone rang, and she hurried to answer it. It was Miss Menzies.

'Morning, Staff. About the twins. I've just been on to the ambulance station at Dornoch and they'll be over here at one o'clock to take the two boys, so if you could see that they have an early lunch et cetera, and please don't forget the small possessions they brought in with them; that's most important.'

Later, when Peter returned, looking fit and wind-swept, his tan deeper now since being out in the fresh air, she told him about the twins. 'I'm not surprised, Laura,' he said quietly, 'but they'll be OK once treat-ment's started. We really can't do a lot more for them here.'

She was busy for the next few hours, Pearl helping, and Janek, in his own way, as he tried to give the two boys a pep talk following Peter's conversation with them. They had received two introductory English les-sons from him and everyone had been amazed at their eagerness to learn and how swiftly they picked up the language.

After they had gone, and lunch was over, on her way to Primrose Laura noticed that Janek was resting with his eyes closed, and caught an expression on Peter's face that looked as if a black thundercloud had drifted across it and stayed there. She could understand his feelings of frustration and helplessness, left sud-denly with nothing to do, yet having left so much behind that needed attention.

She went straight to Baby André; he really was beginning to fill out, and the faint rosiness on his cheeks was now a little deeper, those limpid brown eyes looking so much brighter now. One of the newly appointed part-time nurses, Sarah, stood at her side and took a peep at him. 'Isn't he lovely, Staff? Just look at his hair; even that's taken on a golden shine.'

'He's certainly different from when he first came in. How did he enjoy his bath this morning?'

'Loved it—little hands splashing away like paddles!'

'The other children no trouble?'

'Not really. Their body weight is still abnormal for their height and age, but we're feeding them four times daily with those high-energy milk foods and things,

Mrs Barnard will be in to see them this afternoon. The two teenagers as well.'

'Good. Is Gemma around, by the way? Since she's had to help out in the wards downstairs we haven't seen a lot of each other this week.'

'Well, she did tell me that Miss Menzies wants her up here again from next Monday, especially now some of the patients are being shifted around.'

'OK, thanks; I'll try and meet up with her!'

Peter Wentworth was reading a letter when she returned to Hyacinth. He still looked withdrawn and absorbed in his own affairs, but when she approached he looked up with a wan smile.

'I've had the results of my second medical this morning.' He indicated the letter, which at a quick glance appeared to be three pages of closely packed type. Surely they couldn't have found that much wrong with him?

'I hope its the result you wanted,' she said, not quite understanding the deeply introvert look on his face.

He made a wry grimace. 'Not exactly, Laura.' He pondered for a moment, then explained, 'The board have said they are not, with my present state of health, able to pass me as one hundred per cent fit for the type of work which I'd planned on doing in Eastern Europe. They suggest I see them in six months' time, when they'll review the situation. . .'

CHAPTER FOUR

The silence seemed endless, then Laura said softly, 'I'm so sorry, Peter. I know how much going back meant to you. It must be a sickening disappointment.'

'I can't deny it,' he said, staring into space. 'It's like. . .like leaving a sinking ship.' Then he gave her one of his warm, wry smiles. 'But life is like that; it never does quite what we expect of it.'

A pool of afternoon sunlight flooded the ward suddenly, making her violet-blue eyes seem flecked with a greeny gold as she smiled. 'Well, it can be good or bad,' she said, trying to sound uplifting. 'In this case you may find ultimately that the decision of the board turns out to be a good one. Who knows?'

He grinned unexpectedly, laughter in his eyes now, as well as a small vertical cleft emerging to one side of his firm lips. 'You don't happen to be a soothsayer by any chance, do you?'

She grinned back, seeing a sudden return of the humorous, easygoing man she had come to know. It was a relief, after the varied expressions he'd worn that day that were so unlike him. 'I dabble in a few things,' she quipped, 'and I wouldn't rule out looking into the future!'

'Well, believe it or not, you just did!' He glanced at the letter again, giving her a searching look beneath his lashes, one brow raised in disbelief.

'You're joking, of course?'

'See for yourself. This letter contains far more than I've already related to you. In essence they're more or less suggesting now that I apply for the senior consultant's post here at the Lodge, because, in their words, they think with my knowledge of that part of the world, and the languages I've acquired working there, I'd be extremely useful to them. It would be on an annual contract with a let-out clause to enable me to change my mind, if I wished to do so.'

Laura felt her heart beat faster. What on earth was wrong with her? She hardly knew the man and here she was acting as if. . .as if. . .

Anyway, how could any man make such an impression upon her in such a short time? She took a deep breath to steady her voice. 'Do you want my unbiased opinion?'

'I wouldn't have told you all this if I didn't.'

A little thrill of pleasure went through her at his words. 'Right, well I think it's an extremely sensible and well-thought-out plan. In fact I see no flaw in it, except. . .'

'Yes?'

'Except that the quiet life here may not appeal after the type of existence you've become used to.'

'Agreed. There's just one other thing. The hospital committee has yet to approve the board's suggestion.'

'I would say they have it all cut and dried, and this is a mere formality.'

He appeared pleased with her reply. 'You could be right. Do you know, on reflection I think I'm going to start looking forward to the changes, if they materialise?'

'Fine, Peter! Any further update you need, I'll take a quick peek into my crystal ball!' she laughed as Pearl came in with the laundry trolley to make up the now vacant beds.

'I'll hold you to that,' he said, smiling. 'Meanwhile, I have a few phone calls to make.'

Word soon spread that Mr Wentworth was attending

an important interview at the Lodge a few days later. On the day, the Duke himself, and several other dignitaries connected with the hospital committee, arrived, the five impressive-looking limousines lined up on the drive, their chauffeurs probably in for a long wait.

Two hours later the cars were still there. Laura had been keeping herself busy, and was at present sorting out everything she could see in the large ward linen cupboard—anything to keep her mind off what was happening to Peter.

Pearl returned from a late coffee break, which she'd wanted to have in the servery that morning in order to use the telephone. Gemma suddenly appeared at Laura's shoulder. 'What do you think's going to happen to Mr Wentworth? He's been with those VIPs a jolly long time.'

'I know; difficult to tell. I have the feeling Peter will be disappointed now if he doesn't get the job.'

'Yeah. I think he'll be less friendly if he does, and go all snooty on us!'

'You never know, I——'

Pearl appeared in the corridor just then. 'Mary's just told me that the committee have had coffee, and a light lunch is being taken to them. Maybe they can't agree upon anything?'

Gemma shook her head. 'No, I think Peter's got it. They wouldn't go in for such an elaborate performance had it gone the other way. What do you think, Laura?'

'I'm inclined to think the same as you.'

Pearl, in her usual laid back way, said airily, 'We'll soon know. Mary's going to ring me as soon as the dishes are collected from their room. She'll sense what's going on; it was she who told me to ring her from the servery! Well, we had to know, didn't we?'

Gemma and Laura grinned. 'Listen to that,' Laura said. 'Remind me not to do anything furtive here! Are you sure the bushes aren't bugged, Pearl, so that Mary will give us the word when the cars leave?'

As it happened such extreme measures were not needed. At dinner that evening Miss Menzies announced that Mr Wentworth had been appointed senior consultant at the Lodge, and both she and the staff wished him all the best for the future in his new job.

Applause greeted the statement, and Peter Wentworth rose from his chair, handsome and authoritative in a pale grey suit and university tie. Laura hardly recognised him. His few words of thanks were witty and concise, and on resuming his seat Gemma whispered, 'Wow! He looks tasty.'

Laura said casually, 'He certainly has a more confident air about him.'

Gemma giggled. 'What did I say? He'll soon change; you mark my words.'

When Laura went off duty that evening she realised that there were times when Gemma got on her nerves. Maybe it was she herself that was the problem, she thought charitably; for some reason she was on edge and uneasy, as if Peter's promotion was going to affect her, too.

It was an illogical thought, and there was no reason whatsoever why it should make any difference to her. Any crazy fantasies she'd had about his attractiveness, and the way she was drawn to him, was mere familiarity, which she now had to curb. For one thing, he would most probably be given a doctor's residence, each doctor having his own small flat in a separate house in the grounds, originally built for the Duke's staff for use during the fishing and shooting season.

There would be many subtle changes now their paths would no longer cross: no late evening conversations when the patients were settled for the night, no afternoon discussions on a variety of topics they seemed to have in common, apart from music, which had been absorbing, although there had never been time to go into anything deeply.

In her room she had no inclination to go to bed and read, or watch TV; then she remembered the piano she had seen in an alcove off the common-room. On impulse she wandered down there; there was no one around.

Drawn automatically to the piano stool, she ran her fingers over the piano keys, the instrument a good one and well-tuned. In no time she was indulging in some of her favourite pieces with consummate ease. It was something, a gift perhaps, inherited from her mother, and although Laura had received some training nursing had superseded her eagerness to study music. As ever, her mind drifted away on the melting tones of Debussy, 'Claire de Lune', the notes gradually trailing off, leaving her less tense.

A deep voice said quietly, from the depths of a chair, 'Laura, that was perfect.'

Startled by Peter's remark, she immediately felt a resistance to the usual banter between them; his promotion was changing things. 'Peter,' she smiled, leaving the piano and closing it. 'Oh, I only play for my own amusement.'

He grinned. 'That, along with your psychic powers, fills me with admiration!' He glanced at the sea of empty chairs in the common-room. 'Look, while we're here, let's have a cup of this stuff called coffee out of the machine.'

He placed the plastic cups down as he sat beside her. 'This could be a small celebration, you know, for me, until I can arrange a proper do!'

Laura was gradually relaxing, maybe no longer seeing him as a superior being about to change overnight.

'Thanks, Peter,' she said, taking the coffee from him. 'Many congratulations, anyway.'

'Thank you. I'm not sure I would have done it without your help and encouragement, I might add.'

She looked away, saying quickly, 'You've come through quite a time of it. I think you've done very well.'

'Well, I'd never dreamed of taking on such a job as this, not in this country. I've worked abroad for so long, I'm really still finding my feet.'

'When do the new duties start?'

'This coming Monday. I'll call a meeting before then. But now I'd far rather you told me all about your musical career!'

They discussed the exams she had taken since the age of seven and how she used to dream of becoming a concert pianist until other ambitions took precedence. 'Still,' she said, with a small sigh, 'I shall never give up my love of music; I don't think I could live without it.'

He looked withdrawn suddenly, as if something far removed from this Highland village had claimed him. 'You must never do that, Laura. It's part of life, one of the joys through which we can revive treasured memories and conjure up the beauty of the moment at any time.'

She nodded, a rush of emotion catching at her throat, knowing his thoughts were with so many adults and children whom he had lost or saved in some of the war-ravaged places he had worked, where music so often flourished. 'I believe that too, Peter,' she murmured, then asked, 'Do you play an instrument yourself?' feeling she needed to draw him back from a far distance.

'The piano a little, and when I lived at home I became quite intrigued by the church organ in our village, the vicar at the time thinking I could be of some use helping the choir out! But, as with you, in one's youth there are stars to follow!'

'Definitely! Were you brought up in Scotland?'

'Not really; I was born in South Africa. My father was a ship's surgeon and away quite a bit, but when I was eight my parents thought it time they gave my future some consideration as an only child! That's when we came home to Sussex, where Dad was a village GP, and I spent my formative years at school, then Edinburgh University where Dad went, being a Scot, and ultimately they retired there.'

'I gather you must have had a lust for travel too?'

'Definitely; I couldn't wait to get away. After I'd qualified I spent five years in Kenya at a medical clinic out there, then some time on a cruise ship as the resident doctor; that didn't satisfy me for long, and eventually I made my way back to Paris to the Médicins Sans Frontières, and got caught up with the United Nations and all their problems in Bosnia and Sarajevo. Yet at thirty-five I still have a sense of unachievement.' He grinned. 'Well, perhaps a little less so now, with the new prospects before me!'

Her eyes twinkled. 'Are you quite sure that really is the unexpurgated version?'

He laughed disarmingly. 'Well, I've made a start, anyway!'

When Laura went to bed that night, she sincerely hoped that Peter would not change in his new capacity as senior consultant, but one could never tell.

Peter held his first staff meeting a week after his appointment, flanked at the table in one of the staff-rooms by Miss Menzies, and remaining doctors who could get away. Likewise the nursing staff. There had been a brief résumé from the tall man now speaking so eloquently of his future plans, and his main scheme

—that of forming a specialist team between staff and patients overseen by himself and maybe two doctor colleagues, assisted by nurses with certain experience who would assist in the new venture.

'My aim being,' he said with enthusiasm, 'to keep a continual renewal of patients to be cared for who need treatment of an individual nature because of their background. Children, in particular, will, in a sense, retain a more or less personal doctor and nurse so that confidence is gained on both sides.

'As yet there will be no planned schedule; it may be a question of trial and error, but that will be put right if necessary as we go along.' He smiled. 'But I must stress that teamwork will be the guiding force. Miss Menzies is fully in accord with this. It will be in the nature of an experiment, of course, but I hope one that will become a permanent feature of the Lodge.

'Questions I would welcome. We shall be holding weekly meetings regarding all members of the new team when it is fully formed. Other members of staff will be welcome, so that they know exactly what we are striving for. . .'

That evening Gemma and Laura went for a swim in the indoor pool and afterwards had warm drinks in the balcony shop. Gemma seemed pensive, because she had just that morning received a letter from Ken. 'He's still on about me coming up here,' she told Laura. 'Now that he's going on that course he seems to be blaming me for the time he'll be spending in the States! That's why he rang me that night at that unearthly hour!'

She heaved a huge sigh. 'Honestly, Laura, I sometimes wonder whether falling in love is all it's cracked up to be.' She made a grimace with her pretty mouth. 'Still, perhaps it's the old problem rearing its ugly head again. I'm still not quite as over the moon about him as I might be if we hadn't known each other forever.'

Laura grinned. 'You know your trouble, don't you, Gemma?'

'No, for heaven's sake tell me.'

'Well, I think basically you're both very much in love with each other. It's just the frustration of knowing you can't see each other at all for the next few months. It was different when you were the only one away from home. Now he's suffering too.'

Gemma was looking crestfallen. 'You really think he's realising how much I mean to him, then?'

'That's how it seems to me.'

'Oh, Laura, thanks. I knew you were a real friend from the minute we started talking on the train.' Her deep brown eyes suddenly relieved, she now looked as if she could put her mind to other things; work in particular. 'You know the twelve-year-old on Primrose who looks about eight?' she said suddenly.

'Yes, poor kid. I'm hoping Peter will make her one of his first patients—if she's got the strength for the tests, that is. Sorry, what were you going to say about her?'

'Well, Yasmin, the sixteen-year-old on the ward with her, who seems far more advanced for her age, told me how the younger girl, Nadja, has hardly spoken to her lately, yet they've been the best of friends almost all their lives, living in the same village and going to the same school. She seemed deeply upset about it.'

'Has she any idea why?'

Gemma shrugged. 'Apparently not, but the girl seems really upset. I wondered if you'd like to have a word with Yasmin; perhaps she'd open up a little more to you. She knows enough English to get by.'

'I could, I suppose. Trouble is, Nadja's very young. I mean, the trauma of leaving your own country and the loss of both parents is enough to make anyone clam up.'

'Yes, perhaps we should give it another week or so before we do any more. It might be better if she talked to someone she has confidence in, rather than a stranger.' Gemma pursed her lips. 'Although very often a stranger can make it easier for the sort of thing she might want to talk about. Like losing her parents, whom Yasmin said she adored.'

'True,' Laura murmured thoughtfully. 'Let's hope she opens up to us in a day or two; you never know.' She shook her head sadly. 'Even so, what a hell of a life she now faces.'

The two girls finished their drinks, decided to leave, and gathered up their sports bags. Laura was still pondering on what they had just talked about, when she heard Gemma gasp.

'Wow! Look, isn't that Peter Wentworth poised for a dive?'

Laura looked over the viewing rail; the tall, slim male figure was unmistakably Peter's. As he cut cleanly through the water and did a leisurely but very professional crawl through the blue water, she seemed unable to take her eyes off him; then she remembered Gemma at her side. 'Yes,' she said as coolly as she could. 'Good swimmer.'

Gemma grinned. 'Good diver. Wonder what else he can do?'

Laura turned away from the rail, saying thoughtfully, 'He doesn't appear to be too worried about the scheme he put to us this afternoon. I hope it works out for him.'

'Seems like a jolly good idea. The only snag as far as I see it is if we have enough staff.'

'Well, it's not too bad at present, but if we have another two or three planes in I think we'd be quite unable to deal with the new team as a separate body of staff altogether.'

The following week Peter Wentworth and Miss Menzies got together and produced their list with Mr Lomax, Dr Joan Barnard and two housemen, William Ferguson and a newcomer John McPherson. The nurses were selected, including Gemma and Laura, giving both a boost to their morale. It was a rainy afternoon when Peter sat informally and talked to those who been chosen for the present.

'As I already explained, I want specific children to be allocated to specific medics; nurses in particular will be responsible for much of the detailed work of primary health care. That is to say, health care based on practical, scientifically sound and socially acceptable methods, with the latest technology being made accessible to them.

'As yet, we know little about the patients' actual health needs or the infections in the community from which they come. Some infections may be constantly present, some at certain seasons, such as poliomyelitis, diptheria, measles and whooping cough. We do know that all the children we have here at present are suffering from differing degrees of malnutrition, as well as stress and shock. Without the detailed knowledge we need it is going to take time, observation and care to prepare a suitable programme to meet their health needs.

'As I mentioned before, language barriers, too, are a difficulty. I need hardly say that immunisation is essential, and tests, charts and graphs are needed to establish what has been done. Miss Menzies and I have agreed that we retain Primrose and Hyacinth wards as the "team-wards" for those children who have the health and strength to undergo any treatment or ops urgently needed. But they will be performed only after the most stringent investigations. . .'

It was another hour before the meeting finally ended. To their surprise each person was given a ready-prepared file for every child for whom one, or if necessary two nurses were responsible. Doctors were in overall charge, but mostly working together for complete recovery of the individual patient where possible.

At tea, the team were voluble in their praise of the effective way Peter intended combining health care with certain educational activities—the English language, and one-to-one classes. All in moderate tranquillity, without noise or harassment.

'He deserves to win through,' Dr Barnard said suddenly, to everyone's surprise. 'I only wish there had been someone like him when I was in Jerusalem. During the Hebron mosque massacre, the doctors worked all hours and mostly the mood of near-hysteria seemed to sap all serenity and level-headedness.'

Steven Lomax looked at Joan Barnard, open admiration on his rugged face. 'That must have been one hell of an experience for you, Joan. You'll have to tell us more when you feel up to it.'

Joan Barnard gave the nearest thing to a smile Laura had seen from her. 'That won't be just yet, I'm afraid. It's something of a relief to me to become engrossed in the work here. How much better it is to plan for the future, rather than forever reviving old feuds of the past, killing and maiming because of them.'

By evening the rain had stopped and the gusty wind had blown itself out. Laura decided to go for a walk to dwell upon her new role at the hospital. There was so much to think about. Clad warmly in jeans and anorak, she was glad to breathe in the clean fresh air, with the scent of spring everywhere, even a slight tang of the sea from the small waves of the loch as they met the shore. Briefly she stood, entranced by the scene, the hills like cut-outs against a clear sky, delicate pink from the setting sun.

She walked along the edge of the water, her thoughts returning to Peter Wentworth and the innate strength that emanated from him, despite his obviously harrowing personal experiences abroad. She remembered the night they had talked about music and how relaxed he had seemed then, for a while. Again she pondered on whether he would change eventually with this new job he was taking on. He could no doubt be extremely sardonic when he wanted to. One cold look from those eyes would make one shudder, she thought, and was indicative of the cutting remarks he could deliver.

She shivered suddenly, deciding to turn back when she saw the object of her thoughts strolling towards her. . .

'Laura! This is very pleasant. We obviously both had the same idea!'

She felt the rose colour wash her cheeks, the way he was looking at her. Probably all in her mindless imagination, of course; nevertheless, the warm glow was inside her again. 'Hi! Great minds! It's a pleasant evening now, after the rain.'

'It certainly is.' They strolled back towards the Lodge again. 'Do you know I'm just longing to explore this part of the world?' he said brightly. 'My parents only moved to Edinburgh after I left home. So it's something I'm promising myself one day!'

She looked at him with a perky grin. 'I feel rather the same; it's my first time here, being a southerner! But with all the work you're planning for us there won't be a lot of time for touring!'

He threw back his head in laughter. 'One never knows! There has to be time for living, though, wouldn't you say?' His dark, penetrating, sable-black

eyes met her violet ones. For one heart-stopping
moment she found it impossible to wrench her gaze
away, until he said briskly, 'Coming to a place like this,
Laura, it's a wonderful thing to return to normality.'

'Yes, I imagine so. It must be terrible to witness so
much devastation and killing, yet all the while trying
to heal people again. Although I love nursing, I don't
know if I could bear seeing the unnecessary bloodshed
and sheer cruelty that seems prevalent in the world
just now. Did you not feel that each day you were
fighting a losing battle?'

He stopped suddenly, facing her, that deeply com-
passionate gaze, which had fascinated her from the
very beginning, in his eyes. 'Laura, you would become
hardened as I did. So long as your heart's in the right
place and you know you're helping, so long as the joy
of a small girl's smile wrenches your heart, or the sight
of two wounded people in love who find each other
after thinking they had been parted forever chokes you
up, then those are the defences that safeguard you in
an imperfect world.'

For one crazy moment she wanted to fling both her
arms around him, his quiet, firm voice, the deep
humanity of his words convincing her that should she
marry someone only a fraction like Peter Wentworth
she would be marrying a very good man.

'I'm sorry, Peter; I shouldn't have sounded
so mournful. You, and so many like you, have found
that inner strength which people say we all have.
But it must take the right kind of courage for it to
manifest itself. I should like to think I had a little
of it. . .'

'You have, Laura; be sure of that.'

As the Lodge came into view they walked along in
companionable silence, then parted amicably for their
respective rooms. Laura was glad she didn't have to

share with anyone; she wanted to be pensive and think of many things, until she slept.

The team-wards were becoming well-established. Janek had to be moved downstairs to an orthopaedic ward, much to his disapproval, but, on the promise of everyone visiting him from time to time, decided he'd give it a try. The Primrose babies were left where they were, as well as the two teenage girls. The side-ward was empty, since the three Aids men had been moved, as was Hyacinth, and Miss Menzies had already hinted that another ambulance plane would soon be on its way, when they would need all the extra beds they could spare.

On Thursday afternoon Laura was on Primrose feeding André with his gruel, which he could now take from a spoon. He was propped up with pillows and his huge brown eyes watched her cautiously, as if the next spoonful might not come his way, then, when it did, he smiled, dribbled and smacked his lips all in one. His little limbs were beginning to fill out, and Laura was sure she could see the beginnings of a dimple in one of his knees.

She was putting up André's cot-side when Peter strolled in. He smiled at her, then the baby, gently ruffling the dark curls with one hand and reading his chart with the other. 'He seems to be doing well, you know, Laura. With the basic tests we've managed to do, I don't think there's a lot wrong with him.'

Laura agreed. 'I think he's a tough little fellow.'

Peter hung the chart back, looking across at the other children. The two-year-old little girl lay watching them, cuddling her old toy duck, her large eyes taking everything in. The other young baby was sleeping soundly.

Peter went to Marie's cot, speaking to her in her own language. She laughed, showing him her precious possession. Peter made play with the duck's leg, then gave it back to the child, her little face now animated. Laura referred to her chart, saying, 'She was coughing, apparently, in the night, but after some cough mixture slept well enough. As you can see, she's bright as a button this morning.'

'Yes. We must watch these points, though, Laura; such children go up and down very quickly.'

He crossed the ward to where Yasmin and Nadja lay. Yasmin was sleeping, Nadja leafing idly through a teenage magazine. Peter spoke to the girl gently, evidently asking if she felt better that day. The girl looked embarrassed, turning her face away, shaking her head.

'Has she eaten today, Laura?'

'Yes, only very small portions, though, as usual.'

'I should have thought she'd be glad to talk to me in her own language,' he said, wrinkling his forehead. 'She hasn't complained—to her friend, for instance—of any symptoms in particular that might be worrying her?'

'No. . .' Laura made a quick decision not to mention the discussion she'd had with Gemma. Rightly or wrongly, there seemed no point in scaring the poor child stiff with a barrage of questions for a day or two. 'I'm surprised she's like this with you, Peter,' she said, 'although I've noticed she does seem to have a natural shyness and leaves it to Yasmin to speak for them both.'

Peter nodded, looking at the girl anxiously. 'You could be right, Laura; trouble is, this healing process is not only for the body but for the mind too, which in such circumstances, as we know in this case, is totally unpredictable. Could be tomorrow, could be next year.'

He glanced up at the ward clock. 'I think I'll have to

leave seeing the rest. We've a member of the hospital committee turning up this afternoon for a chat to see how the new teamwork is going.' He gave a grin. 'I suspect it's to see how the new senior consultant is doing too! I have a horrible feeling that a great deal of my work will be admin, and that's not really my idea of healing!'

'Early days yet!' she said cheerfully. 'Provided the next ambulance plane doesn't arrive in the next few hours I think we might be fairly organised. You might even be able to delegate some of that office work!'

'What would I do without you, Laura?' he grinned, then walked away, leaving her pondering upon those words.

Next afternoon, one of the nurses recruited from downstairs to the team on Primrose and Hyacinth came hurrying up to Laura. Molly James was big, bouncy and Irish, never seeming to have a care in the world, but at present looked quite concerned.

'Laura, I don't want to worry you but Nadja seems unhappy today. It's just that apart from her mournful face she has big dark rings under her eyes, and Yasmin tells me her friend has "a big ache in her head".'

'OK, thanks, Molly; I'll get some pain-killers for you to give her, *if* she'll take them. But don't press it if she's adamant. I'll try and get hold of Mr Wentworth.'

'Right. Any fresh news from Ann Weekes?'

'Not yet, no. Could be some time, I think.'

Laura rang Morag, the secretary, to put a call out for Mr Wentworth to come up to Primrose when he could. She carried on with writing her day report, then her own specific patients' file. The patients that had been allocated to her were André and Nadja, and every detail about them had to be recorded in detail daily.

Peter came into the office, with what she could only describe as a crumpled look on his face. 'Morag said you wanted me,' he said brusquely.

'Yes, it's Nadja. . . .' She repeated Molly's words.

'You say you gave her paracetamol?'

'Yes. She's had them before when she was first admitted without any ill effect.'

He pushed a hand through his thick dark hair. 'I see. Well, I think tomorrow the girl will have to have a thorough medical. She hasn't yet had one because of her nervous disposition and we wanted her to settle in, but we'll make this for ten tomorrow morning. Is there anything else?'

'No, thank you.'

'Right. If anyone else wants me I'm out. You might also inform Morag of that fact, please.'

Laura stared at the door through which Peter Wentworth had passed without another word.

Had the person whom she had so recently placed high upon a pedestal now developed feet of clay. . .?

CHAPTER FIVE

DESPITE Peter's mood change, over what seemed to Laura a perfectly normal discussion between them regarding Nadja, the following morning all seemed peace and tranquillity. He had been on the phone to her earlier about some test analyses and sounded quite pleasant.

It was the time when drugs, TPRs, baths, dressings and bedsore-prevention treatment were seen to, beds remade and flowers returned to the wards, followed by the mid-morning drinks trolley arriving, with daily newspapers for those who wanted them. This air of comforting domesticity reached Laura in the office where she was completing forms for various replacements, when the atmosphere was completely shattered by a most terrifying scream, causing her to leap from her chair and hurry into the ward.

Molly was attempting to prevent a frantic Yasmin from jumping out of bed to reach Nadja, who was moaning with an almost animal intensity and throwing herself from side to side in her bed. Yasmin, in a near hysterical state, was trying to explain what was wrong, but no one could understand her.

'I'll ring for Mr Wentworth. Molly, you get someone to give you a hand,' Laura said swiftly. The noise was nerve-racking as she raised her voice to make herself heard on the phone, all protocol forgotten as Peter's voice reached her. 'Peter, can you come immediately, please? I'm not sure if Nadja might be having an epileptic fit. It's upsetting the others, I'm afraid.'

In minutes he appeared on the ward. Nothing had

78

changed, except that both young girls now seemed to be vying with each other to see who could make the most noise; even Peter's presence made no difference. He attempted to calm Yasmin and spoke rapidly to her, the girl sobbing, then quietening a little while pointing to Nadja, who was still moaning, with tears pouring down her cheeks. Once satisfied that Yasmin was in no real trouble, Peter turned his attention to Nadja, who broke out into a fresh paroxysm of crying and wailing when he came anywhere near her, pulling up the bedcovers as if to hide herself.

Peter said suddenly, 'Screens, please, Nurse.' Molly put them in place while Laura turned back the covers against Nadja's will, her hands white across the knuckles with the grip she had on them. Peter stepped forward then and muttered, 'Oh, dear, the poor kid; so that's what she was so worried about.'

Laura looked down at the blood-smeared nightgown and sheet. 'Her periods. . .'

The child was screaming hysterically now.

'We need to give her a small injection to calm her; Omnopon should do it,' Peter said quickly.

Once Nadja was drowsy, Laura and Molly cleaned the girl up, remade the bed, and explained what the sanitary pad was for; afterwards Laura sent Molly to prepare a warm drink for the girl. When all was quiet again Peter explained to Nadja in her own language what had happened; she obviously knew very little about her own body.

Later, in the office, the emergency over, he seemed somewhat withdrawn as Laura poured tea for him, then he said curtly, 'You know, Laura, this business with Nadja has to be of great concern to all of us regarding young girls of this age. Coming from a different culture and upbringing as they do, what to us is a normal and natural situation can be more complicated for them, and this simply must be taken into consideration. I suggest that, with Miss Menzies' agreement, you use Nadja as a case history in the future, so that your nurses can be on the alert with teenage patients.'

Laura pursed her lips. 'Yes, I agree,' she said tersely. Surely he wasn't blaming her for this incident?

'Shock can cause havoc with such bodily cycles, especially under the sort of terrible conditions some of these youngsters have had to put up with——' Peter stopped speaking suddenly, noticing the sudden look of annoyance on Laura's face. 'I'm not blaming you, Laura, but as this is a hospital for internationals we must be one step ahead the whole time.' He stood up to leave. 'So you will see Miss Menzies when you can?'

'Certainly, and I'll include your comments in Nadja's file report,' she answered curtly.

As if having second thoughts, he paused at the door, turning to look at her, a perplexed look on his face. 'You see, Laura, if you'd had some hands-on experience in these war-zones, you may have identified the reason for Nadja's misery.' His tone was half-apologetic, half-censorious.

So she was right. He was getting at her. With great restraint she kept her cool.

'I take your point, Peter; it should put us all on our guard in future.' Her lovely eyes blazed suddenly. 'Nevertheless, I get the feeling at times that you consider we are extremely naïve here in comparison with your own record abroad. As a matter of fact, I joined a separate heavy-lorry supply load into Bosnia last year, and although I only spent a short period of time there after distribution it was enough to make me only too aware of the real suffering and starvation that existed, as it was the depths of winter out there. As a result, my thoughts are never far away from those people.'

She drew a deep breath, and then spoke quietly, without any sense of retaliation. 'Not exactly "hands-on" in your book, but an extremely levelling experience in mine.'

His expression was difficult to define; the dark eyes searched hers for a brief second, then he said in a low monotone, 'I see. I should like to hear more about it some time.'

She was glad when he had gone, and already rather regretted telling him what she had. It would, of course, make no difference to his thoughts on Nadja, but saying what she had, irrelevant or not, acted as something of a safety-valve to her deeper feelings about her brother.

Dragging her thoughts back to her desk work, she thought she would certainly bring the subject up at one of their weekly meetings for discussion by the team, to see what they thought. Wasn't that what Peter had hinted at in his initial setting up of the group? That it was to be trial and error as they became used to the differing circumstances under which they worked? It was a new attitude to medicine that reflected the changing times—for instance teenage girls like Nadja having to endure such privations during what should have been the best days of their lives.

She went off duty, impatient with herself for dwelling on the situation any further; she would only get steamed up again, and that helped no one. As she went upstairs she happened to meet Joan Barnard, who greeted her quite warmly, and instinct made Laura ask, 'Dr Barnard, could I have a word with you, just for a few minutes?'

Joan Barnard's lined face wreathed into a quiet smile. 'Of course. It's Laura, isn't it?'

'Yes, Laura Meadows.'

'Let's go along to my flat. I'm dying for a cup

of tea; I expect you can do with one too!'

'That's very kind of you, but I don't want to put you to any trouble. . .'

'It's no trouble; in fact I'm rather glad of the excuse to invite you here,' she said as they entered the very comfortable flat. 'I know it's silly but I feel rather the odd one out amidst so many pretty young things these days! When I was in Hebron there were so many dreadful things going on, I don't think any of us thought of such comparisons. Here it's so peaceful, and it comes as rather a surprise to realise I'm so ancient! Sit down, my dear; I'll put the kettle on.'

In cushioned chairs, sipping their tea and deciding not to indulge in biscuits with dinner only half an hour away, Laura told Joan Barnard of the incident with Nadja.

'I'm afraid I blew my top when Mr Wentworth hinted, albeit subtly, that I should have foreseen the young girl's development. As it happened, even her best friend Yasmin didn't know about it. The girl had been very secretive and, well, we all thought we were doing as much as we could for her.'

The woman nodded thoughtfully. 'Well, I'm not going to say it's typical of a man, but something close to it! After all, we still don't know how much the girl had suffered and to what degree. I dare say we shall have to make sure that Peter, or even myself, has to have regular sessions of counselling with her; that I believe to be absolutely essential. Again, it's what we tried to do in the hospital I came from, but among the wounded young people we had to cope with the onset of female puberty was, I'm sure, the last thing on any of our minds.'

Laura gave a sigh. 'You've made me feel much better, Dr Barnard. You just seemed to be the right person to tackle about this; I only hope you don't think

I've overstepped the mark in approaching you.'

'Not a bit of it.' Joan Barnard glanced at her wrist-watch. 'Come along to dinner now, Laura; you're applying far too much anxiety to it. Nevertheless,' she added as they went downstairs together, 'I hope you'll come up and see me again whenever you want to.'

Laura smiled. 'It's great of you; thank you.'

Happily she had the feeling that the lady she and Gemma had thought so saturnine and remote was going to be 'one of them' after all.

The minute Laura walked into the office next morning she knew something was wrong. An air of silence, a brooding sense of distress prevailed. Night Sister was sitting at the desk with the night report open in front of her, her face white, but not with tiredness.

'What's wrong with everyone this morning?' Laura asked quickly as one of the night nurses turned hurriedly and left the room.

'Bad news, I'm afraid, Laura. Little Nadja died in her sleep.'

'Oh, no! It can't be true.'

'I'm afraid it is. Both Mr Wentworth and Mr Lomax rushed over here to her in the night. They thought she'd had some kind of heart attack, but it wasn't that; she just seemed to fade away. They're talking to Miss Menzies now. It's hit us all for six, I can tell you.'

'Oh, my God! And after all the girl's been through. What about Yasmin?'

'She's hardly said a thing. I think these children are so used to coping with death it no longer hits them in a way we understand, but we'll have to make sure she's well cared for—something's going to give sooner or later.'

A rap on the door brought in Peter, tall and gaunt. 'Morning, Laura. You've heard the news?'

She nodded, tears not far away. 'Yes, I can't take it in.'

'Neither can any of us. At present we're still saying it was heart failure, and last night's incident had some bearing on it; I'm convinced of that.'

Laura tried to forget the conversation she'd had with Peter the night before, and said quietly,

'Once Yasmin has recovered from this loss we're really going to have to try and find out from her if there's something we still don't know.'

'Too early yet, Laura; it'll have to wait.'

Laura opened her mouth to speak, then decided not to.

The entire Lodge remained under a cloud, young Nadja's death affecting everyone badly. Two days later, Molly James searched Laura out while she was labelling up urine samples.

'It's Yasmin, Staff; she says she wants to speak to you and Mr Wentworth.'

Peter joined Laura, and they went into Primrose ward where Molly had set out two chairs at Yasmin's bedside, and drawn the curtains around the bed. Yasmin was sitting up, not quite so distraught, but very miserable, and clutching an opened envelope in her hand. She had apparently found it in Nadja's bedside locker, addressed to herself. Peter gave her a gentle smile. 'You wanted to tell us something, Yasmin?' he said as they sat down.

She nodded, handing him the envelope.

'Are you sure you want us to read this?'

Tears filled her eyes for the first time. 'Yes. . .yes.'

Peter read the childish hand, a nerve working at his temple, his face grim. For a moment he said nothing to Yasmin, except to say that they would be back shortly to talk to her.

In the office, Peter leaned against the desk, the letter

having obviously had a devastating effect upon him. He unfolded it, saying, 'I will translate Nadja's words as best I can, Laura.' He began:

'My dearest friend Yasmin,

When you read this letter, I will no longer be in this terrible world. But I must tell you why we have not been able to speak together as we used to. You remember when the soldiers came to our village and my parents were killed, among others. I was hiding in our loft but was soon found, and told to go to my bedroom, all the furniture burnt because of the cold. They had been drinking, Yasmin, and they flung me on the floor and did terrible things to me which I did not understand. Afterwards I was left bleeding. I did not know what had happened because my parents had never told me these things. I had heard of rape at school long ago and perhaps that's what it was. I could not speak of this to anyone, even you. I was too ashamed.

'My secret made me feel dirty; the bleeding would go for a while and then come back. When we came to Scotland I was afraid the doctors would find out and I did not know what to do. On that bad day Mr Wentworth said he was to examine me, the blood was there again. I thought it was because of what the soldiers had done and they had made me ill. I was so afraid, I could not stop myself from screaming and screaming and I wanted my mother. I longed to sleep forever. I am sorry that I spoilt our friendship, dear Yasmin. We were happy once; please do not forget those days we had together. I feel ill in a way I cannot express. Perhaps the day will come when I shall see my beloved parents again. I will not mind. One day I pray you will return to our country again. Your ever devoted friend, Nadja.'

Peter made no comment, leaving a poignant silence between them. Laura's throat had closed and she could not speak as tears filled her eyes. 'There's just nothing we can say, is there?' she whispered brokenly, biting her lower lip, reaching for her handkerchief.

He was shaking his head, his eyes like stones. 'My God, those murdering thugs. . .'

Later, when they talked to Yasmin, the girl seemed more at ease discussing Nadja's troubles. 'If only she had said something to me about it. She was a baby really, being brought up as an only child. Her parents were shy, gentle people; they would not have told their daughter the things she should have known. I could not because I knew she would be upset and her parents, I think, would have disapproved of me.'

Laura smiled wanly at Yasmin. 'That poor young girl's burden was far too heavy to carry. From now on, Yasmin, you must promise to talk to us about anything that's bothering you. I know you're four years older than Nadja, but don't shut us out. We're here to help you.'

Peter nodded approval, saying little, no doubt feeling that it was for Laura to convince Yasmin of their compassion and understanding at such a time.

Once they were both assured that the girl was now coming out of the first brunt of the shock she had sustained and beginning to show signs of her natural level-headedness, Molly took over. She brought her a warm milky drink with some of the biscuits she liked, Laura suggested that she sit with the girl for a while to talk about anything she wished, or just remain at her bedside, Molly telling her about Ireland and the beauties of County Down, which was her home.

Peter later accompanied Laura to lunch, as if he was in a protective mood towards her, yet neither said a great deal, except that, while drinking coffee, he asked,

'Laura, do you feel up to going out for a drink tonight?'

She was appalled at the way her heart leapt so quickly at the question, when she was so low-spirited over Nadja. His hand was suddenly covering hers, her hesitation obviously making him conclude quite the opposite to what she was feeling, as he said with concern, 'Only, that is, if you really want to. I felt it might take your mind off Nadja for a while.'

She smiled, and he thought the curve of her lips was far superior to any artist's impression. 'It's very kind of you, Peter; it would probably be quite a sensible idea.'

His eyes had regained the sparkle that now erased the strain from his face. 'I'll meet you outside at eight, then, if that's OK.'

'Fine, I'll be there.'

They drove out to a small hostelry on the outskirts of Brora. It was a calm evening, with hardly any wind off the sea, the loch still and silvery. After the first few minutes of getting underway, they talked of their love of the countryside, the wildlife in that particular part of Scotland of which they both knew so little.

Peter laughed suddenly. 'Wouldn't it be marvellous to take a whole fortnight off, just to explore this wonderful area alone?'

'I often think the same. Just think of having a horse and gypsy caravan painted scarlet to do such a trip! I believe it's possible to hire them, rather like canal barges. Both modes of transport seem so peaceful.'

They pulled up outside a small stone building with a solid slate roof, white-washed walls and brilliantly packed window-boxes spilling over with colour. He got out of the car and opened her door. 'If it's as good inside as it looks out here, we're going to be OK.'

Warmth and friendliness greeted them, and they settled in an alcove that boasted a padded oak settle beneath a window that overlooked a vista of pine trees, opening out to a small sandy shore at the far end of the loch.

They settled for wine, and inevitably their conversation turned to Nadja. Peter stared into his wine-glass, saying quietly, 'Laura, one of the other reasons I wanted you to come out like this tonight was to apologise for my heavy-handed remark about Nadja. I realised afterwards what an insensitive thing it was to say; it was outrageous of me to think that you or anyone else could have gauged what had happened when we all had so much else to think about.'

He gave a long sigh. 'I often think my own problems may be clouding my judgement. . .' He twirled the near-empty glass between his long, slim fingers, deep in contemplation, as if trying to make a decision of some kind.

Laura guessed he was beset by his own affairs, and felt she hadn't the right to prompt him. Eventually he continued, 'When I was in Bosnia, I saw dreadful things, things I certainly wouldn't want you to know about—and in many ways I feel that poor little Nadja has been blessed to be taken in some respects. She had suffered and seen much, and at such an impressionable age she would never have wholly recovered.'

'You're probably right, Peter, but nevertheless it seems so heartless that she and so many other young people should have their lives so cruelly and brutally ended——' She broke off, a dry sob tearing at her throat as the full import of what she had said dawned upon her.

'Laura, my dear, please don't,' he said, seeing the tears in her eyes brim over. He handed her an immaculately laundered handkerchief, with which she dabbed her cheeks.

'So sorry, Peter; it's just that today has been rather

a strain for me. I should never have mentioned *my* trip to Bosnia in the first place, only, you see. . .'

She told him how her brother had insisted she accompany him, and how determined he had been to return there to work, once having had the results of his exams. She went on to tell him of the subsequent tragedy, and how it marked the beginning of her parents' marriage break-up and the divorce that was pending. Her bottom lip quivered as her voice trailed away, yet to some extent she felt very much better having talked about it.

Peter's face had been full of sympathy as he'd listened to her, and now he said gently, 'Laura, if there's only one thing that coming home has done for me it's realising how, even without war, people still suffer. Somehow, in the midst of gunfire and bombs dropping, one tends to forget that unpleasant things are still taking place in the outside world.'

Gradually they returned to less harrowing topics, and later, as they walked back to the car, he took her arm protectively, and the closeness of him made her feel utterly safe from the harshness of life, if only for a few short moments.

When they got back to the Lodge, he walked with her to the nurses' entrance. Stopping at her door, he smiled down at her. 'A million thanks for this evening, Laura; I've enjoyed it immensely.'

'I certainly have.'

'I hope, too, that you've now forgiven this thoughtless, intolerant male?'

She smiled, not realising how, to the man watching her, the soft glow of moonlight enhanced the attractive features of her face, briefly banishing the emptiness of despair from his heart—something he had thought would never happen. Laura wondered what he was thinking and said, with a slight tilting of her head, as their eyes met, 'It's been a lovely evening, Peter, and please forget our. . .misunderstanding. I reacted just as badly. We've all been on edge recently. Perhaps once Nadja's funeral's over it will be easier.'

He lifted her hand to his lips then, kissing the back of its velvety smoothness. 'Who knows? Maybe we can do the same again some time in happier circumstances.'

Two mornings later Nadja, after a simple ceremony, was laid to rest in the hillside cemetery of the tiny church of St Callans. Buried in the midst of a widespread, Highland crofting community, she would not be alone.

News had travelled fast about the girl, and, as well as the Duke and Duchess attending, people came from far and wide, and Nadja's grave was awash with spring flowers. It was a bright morning, white clouds scudding across a blue sky as if a new beginning was in store for the young Bosnian who had seen few springs in her own lifetime. Yasmin, too, conducted herself bravely and with dignity. After dropping two red roses on to her friend's coffin, she left with her loving memories.

It was another two weeks before the pall of melancholy began to lift somewhat from the Lodge. Miss Menzies gave Yasmin a small side-ward of her own, now that the girl's health was improving, and the joy on Yasmin's face was ample reward for them all.

As if to draw them back to reality Miss Menzies then informed them that a planeload of patients would be arriving the following day. She looked at the anxious faces of Gemma and Laura. 'Don't worry, you two, it will probably not affect the teamwork people at present. Certainly not in the first instance, anyway. Mr Wentworth may subsequently have to take one or two urgent cases up to Hyacinth, but that's why it's standing empty at present.'

Miss Menzies was quite right—the new intake of patients did not affect them directly, except that they were then told it might not be too long before another plane arrived. Molly was busily sorting out bedlinen in the ward linen cupboard when Laura repeated this message from Miss Menzies.

'She'll have to get more staff,' Molly said in her direct fashion. 'We may have had a few extra recruits in, but it won't be enough at this rate. I suppose the point is not everyone wants to come to such an isolated spot.'

'That's understandable,' Laura murmured, checking her laundry list against the steadily rising pile of pillow-cases that Molly was counting. 'By the way, did you know that, apart from our swimming-pool, we're soon to have a real sports centre with proper equipment?'

'Well, they've got to keep us going somehow, haven't they?'

They finished the job just as it was time for first lunch, and Laura dispatched Molly and Pearl. She remained in the office to see to the day's menus needed for her patients. She was surrounded by paper when there was a brisk tap on the door and Peter walked in.

'You look busy,' he grinned, glancing at her desk.

'Just a little. Can I help?'

He had crossed the room to gaze out of the window at the rather grey morning. 'Misty out there at the moment; it's hardly possible to see the other side of the loch. . .'

His back view was as attractive as his front, she thought, broad shoulders thrust back, dark hair curling thickly to the nape of his neck behind, immaculate dark suit apparently bought on a recent trip to Inverness. . .

He turned round suddenly, long, slim legs planted firmly, with an almost schoolboyish, defiant stance against the world and its problems, and gave her a pensive smile. 'Sorry, I was miles away. . . Yes, I think you could help, actually. . .'

The faintly Scottish lilt in the deep voice, plus the fact that he was now leaning towards her from the other side of her desk, resting on his hands, face close enough for her to be disturbingly aware of shaving lotion and talc, made her forget everything else.

'Now, last night Steve Lomax and I were talking about extending membership of our potential club with some kind of regular musical recitals. . .'

'Oh, I thought you hadn't come in for a cup of tea!' she laughed. 'No, sorry, count me out!'

'Now come on, Laura; you can play the piano, and we can organise small concerts for the patients!'

'No, Peter!'

'Pity; I've already put your name forward.'

'You can take it back again, then,' she said briskly. 'I shall only make a fool of myself in front of a lot of people. Just because I had ambitions to be a concert pianist, it doesn't turn me into one.'

He sat on the corner of her desk. 'I told Steve I'd have a fight on my hands, but I'm sorry to tell you neither Steve nor I will take no for an answer. We'll get this concert party together if it kills us.'

'That's a bit extreme, in my opinion. OK, then, if it's a matter of life and death, but don't blame me if things go horribly wrong.'

'That's what I like—a girl full of optimism!'

After Peter had gone it was difficult to concentrate on the menus. If this plan went ahead it meant they would be thrown together more often, which in itself would not have bothered her, were it not for the fact that his closeness always produced an immediate frisson of excitement within her, which irritated and intrigued her in one.

It had never happened to her before. Yes, there had been light flirtations in the two other general hospitals in which she'd worked following her training, and in fact when she had foolishly thought herself in love with her air-steward boyfriend it had been rather a novelty getting to know someone not directly connected with her working-day life.

But this present situation was quite different. She was sure the attraction was on her side only, and yet here she was acting like a lovesick schoolgirl. Perhaps this whole business would work in two ways, nevertheless. Maybe if she met Peter socially more often the glow would fade, and she would discover he was just a mere mortal with ordinary failings, like any other human being. In fact, she had thought just that when he had been so cutting about Nadja, but the trouble was she so quickly forgave him, and then the attraction crept back again. . .

'Laura, you're doing Chopin's Waltz in G Flat Major, aren't you?'

Four nights later Steven Lomax and Peter were well underway with their plans. About ten members of staff had volunteered to take part and Laura nervously contributed her piece, which ended on a burst of spontaneous applause that made her beam with pride. Cups of tea were served all round when the auditions were over, and Peter came up to her with a smile of admiration.

'I'm telling you, Laura, the world has lost a potential star in you!'

She grinned. 'And your rendering from *Peer Gynt* on the ivories was second to none! And now the flattery stakes are over, you don't take sugar, do you?'

she asked, balancing a tray filled with cups.

'Not for me, thanks. Let me take that from you, then I'll flatter you some more!'

Everyone was slightly over the top with the feeling of achievement that evening, and they set a provisional date for the first concert. Dennis had surprised them all by playing a small electronic keyboard; a friend of his played the drums, Gemma strummed a guitar, and Pearl burst into soul singing and anything else the members demanded.

As Laura went up to bed that night she felt that the Lodge was springing to life in a way that she had never predicted.

CHAPTER SIX

NEXT day Peter examined one of the babies on Primrose whose parents had been missionaries before being brutally murdered in a South African riot. A beautiful child, with the happiest of smiles, he was eighteen months old, and named Tiki, after the smallest coin in South Africa, because he had been so small at birth. All this information came from Peter, who had come to hear about the baby through the Red Cross.

Now Tiki was showing signs of diphtheria. He had been isolated in a side-ward for the last three days and, although Dennis had been assigned to look after him as one of his two individual teamwork patients, two other nurses had been brought in for rota nursing in an endeavour to prevent the infection spreading.

The examination completed, Dennis and Peter discarded their masks and gowns as they returned to the office, faces serious.

'There's no doubt, I would say, that the child's a victim of this killer disease. He has a low-grade fever and cries constantly with pain of one kind or another,' Peter said disconsolately. 'We'll just have to do the best we can for him in his frail state.'

'It's a damned shame; he was doing so well with his improved intake of the right food, but, like you, I see it as an uphill struggle.'

Laura came in then, surveying them both with raised eyebrows. 'Well, hi! I must say neither of you two looks full of the joys of that splendid spring outside.' She smiled, having just returned from a walk in the pine woods behind the Lodge, after an early lunch.

'It's little Tiki, Laura. I'm practically certain he's in for diphtheria. As you know, incubation period can take one to six days and we were just hoping we were wrong, but we'll take throat swabs now and get confirmation.'

'Oh, Lord; what type do you think it might be?'

'I would say laryngeal; he already has a dry cough, and that's not the best of signs.' Peter turned at the door on leaving. 'We won't wait for the result of the swabs; I want to begin treatment immediately. I've seen this scourge so often.'

'Is it to be penicillin?'

'Yes, procaine; it's less soluble so there's slow release and absorption from the intramuscular site.'

Dennis shook his head as Peter went on his way. 'Astute guy, that. At first I simply thought the child had developed a common cold as he'd sneezed several times too.'

'He's good with children, there's no doubt about that,' Laura said, busying herself at the drugs cupboard, and preparing the syringe dish for the baby.

'So, how did you enjoy being a musical celebrity last night, then?' Dennis grinned.

Laura blushed. 'Oh, Dennis, don't you start! My old piano teacher would have had a fit if she'd heard me!'

'Modesty's OK in its place, Laura, but a little bit of faith in your own abilities doesn't go amiss, you know! Well, I'm off duty in an hour, so I think I'll mug up on the really stunning performance I intend giving next week!'

'Bully for you,' she grinned. 'Nice to be some people!'

On Saturday morning Laura had a busy time as it had been confirmed that little Tiki had contracted diphtheria, and inevitably there was great concern that the other small baby in Primrose might have it also. So far there had been no signs. They had begun a diphtheria antitoxin regime, starting with a sensitivity test before administering the antitoxin. Laura was giving Pearl Peter's instructions.

'We want 0.1 ml of 1 in 1000 dilution of antitoxin intracutaneously. If it's a sensitive case there may be an eruption of the skin. Let me know, will you? I'll be doing André's tests.'

André seemed to be retaining his slow but good progress. He was such a sweet-natured child and always had a smile for everyone. Having finished recording his chart, Laura was re-fastening the side of the cot when Peter appeared, smiling, and headed straight for the cot. The baby was equally happy to see Peter, and his little feet seemed to pump up and down with joy. 'What a young rascal you are!' Peter laughed, but with great tenderness.

Laura thought she had never seen a man with such gentle compassion for every child he met. 'He's doing very well, Peter,' she said.

'He is. Although we have to be very careful with these infections that are starting to appear now. Let's hope Tiki's diphtheria is not going to be a bad attack. Laryngeal is one with some of the worst complications.'

'So I believe. . .'

They were still talking when Pearl returned to tell them that the baby she was dealing with had shown negative signs of sensitivity.

'Thank heaven for that, Pearl,' Peter muttered. 'Right, now the remaining antitoxin should be given intravenously and slowly. Epinephrine, 1 in 1000 solution should be kept ready in a syringe, and given intravenously in the case of a reaction.'

From two o'clock that afternoon Laura had the rest of the day off. It had been drizzling with rain intermittently all morning, but now the sun was scattering the clouds away and she bowled along on her bicycle to buy a few necessary items she wanted from the village. She felt an enormous sense of freedom as she rode along the loch path, sunlight dappling the water to one side; spring green tipping the pine branches on the other. She couldn't imagine a better place to be at the moment.

With her shopping completed and her regular tour around the antique shops over, she was about to collect her bicycle when she was sure she saw Peter drawing up at one of the larger hotels. She could be mistaken, because she had no idea he owned a car, but remembered him telling her that he hired a vehicle whenever he needed to go into Inverness or anywhere beyond Brora.

But she was not mistaken. While she was rather rudely staring across the road at him, he waved and, getting out of the car, came nimbly towards her. 'Hi, Laura! Come and have a look at this!'

She duly admired the new silver-grey BMW. 'Very nice too,' she beamed up at him, brilliant sunlight catching her hair. 'You definitely need something to get around in. After all, weren't you talking about visiting your parents in Edinburgh?'

'Indeed, when I can get round to it. Anyhow——' he smiled down at her—'now that you're here, how about letting me buy you tea in the hotel there? I'd almost given up the idea of having it alone.'

'I'd love to. What about my bike?'

'That's no problem! I'll take it back in the boot with us.'

'Oh, no, that's sacrilege!'

'Tell you what, I'll get one of the hospital van chaps to come in and collect it tomorrow; they're always up and down here.'

'OK, then, if you're sure.'

'Definitely. Let's have a touch of luxury for once!'

Laura only realised that it was a sumptuously appointed five-star hotel once they were inside. They sat in a discreet alcove over damask and silver, eating wafer-thin sandwiches, pâté and anchovies on slivers of toast, and they had a choice of teas, finding a mutual liking for Earl Grey, and delectable pastries of the melt-in-the-mouth variety.

Sitting back when they had finished, and everything had been whisked away, Peter talked to her about his experiences abroad, then, rather to her surprise, moved on to more personal and poignant topics. He sat back easily in the comfortable wing chair opposite her, his angular face, with its aristocratic calm, only revealing his true feelings by a sudden turbulence in his dark eyes when he talked of the girl he loved.

'She was working with the Red Cross too, Laura. We were ecstatically happy. Her family background was medical but by profession she was a cellist with a classical music education, and from time to time gave recitals, whenever it could be arranged. Because she wanted to help, through the Red Cross she was able to assist with a certain amount of first aid and generally do whatever she could. She had a sister too, but did not speak of her very often.

'Anyway, she and her parents were in a bombed area when a damaged building collapsed, and they all died at the same time.'

Laura stared at him, a far greater understanding of him now dawning upon her. The sudden outbursts of irritability, the dark silences that at times seemed to shut out the rest of the world, then the sudden change when he was so gently reasonable to everyone—all of that made sense now.

She murmured, almost beneath her breath, 'I am so

sorry, Peter, I had no idea. . .and yet perhaps I would be less than honest if I didn't say you appeared to carry an invisible burden, which I put down to the misery and death you had witnessed in those warring countries.'

'Partly yes, Laura, but it was Marika's death that was such a terrible blow for me, and now there's only my deep love of music that can still link us together.'

He stopped talking briefly, then, after a pause, went on, 'Please don't take that as meaning that I intend living the rest of my life in the past. I don't. And I find it very strange that you should also have a great feeling for the world of music. I can tell you that when I first heard you play—and I mean this——' his dark eyes regained their twinkle '—I could hear the spark of something special there, something dedicated, and that's why you must continue.'

They carried on discussing books and the theatre, time just melting away. Later, sitting at his side in the car, Laura felt that they reached the Lodge far too soon. It was quite dark by then, and a misty rain had returned with the night, so enhancing her sense of being completely alone with him as they drew up outside the Lodge. He turned to look at her, his face, in the shadows, almost that of a stranger, yet softer in some way against the faint light now glimmering from the reflection of stars in the loch.

'Thank you, Laura; that was one of the nicest trips I've had for many a day. I hope it was for you too?'

'Without doubt.' She smiled softly. 'And thank *you*, Peter.'

He drew her firmly into his arms at that moment and she could not resist; she was far too willing. Her heart beat wildly and her lips responded to his kiss, which seemed to seal a bond of friendship between them—for that, she told herself breathlessly, was all it could be.

'Not every girl would be so generous as to listen to my problems, Laura.' He smiled, his arms dropping gently from her as if to break the tension between them. She felt sure he'd noticed that her reaction had been more passionate than he'd intended it to be when he said in that low, beautiful voice, 'Your friendship means a great deal to me, Laura; thank you again.'

In a daze of emotion, she moved towards the door, hardly realising that Peter was already outside to give her a hand from the car. She stepped out, her slim yet curvaceous figure outlined by the pale blue jersey wool dress she had hurriedly put on that afternoon beneath her waterproof jacket, as a change from jeans. Peter was saying, 'I hope you enjoy the rest of your evening off. I have to go back to the ward now to see how young Tiki is, so I'll see you tomorrow.' His eyes met hers. Nothing more was said between them, and he turned from her quickly and got back into the car.

She spent the rest of the evening reliving the occasion. She had no inclination to speak to anyone; the outing had been one she would never forget, especially the kiss.

It was not until next day that Laura remembered Peter saying they might go to a concert some time in Inverness. She had agreed with pleasure. 'I know they quite often have visiting international stars here in Scotland,' she had said. 'In the main cities, that is.' She had also wondered, rather flippantly, whether Peter would be able to leave André, while he was some eighty miles away. He had such a soft spot for the child. But then so did she, and the rest of the staff. At least it revealed again the depth of his compassion, despite the edge of bitterness he felt because of his lost love.

Laura's thoughts were never far from Peter that day, but she hardly saw him.

Miss Menzies kept her finger on the pulse of things and had regular meetings of various kinds with different groups of staff, including Peter, even if occasionally it had to be during off-duty time. With recruitment continuing, gradually a pattern was emerging which kept Primrose and Hyacinth wards and its staff separate from the rest of the running of the establishment.

It was in this regard, while Gemma and Laura were having coffee in the servery, that Gemma suddenly said, 'Miss Menzies is planning to promote another staff nurse to sister. Did you know?' Laura appeared not to have heard. 'Hey, Laura, you look a bit out of this world this morning; what were you up to last night?' Gemma had a habit of jumping from one thing to another.

Laura hoped her blush wasn't too obvious. 'I had an early night, as a matter of fact; don't you often find the more sleep you have, the worse you feel next day?'

'Come to think of it, yes. Anyway, to get back to this promotion thing, what do you think?'

'I honestly don't know,' Laura answered, the instant thought flashing through her head that if she applied and obtained the job she would probably be removed from the team, which in turn meant no longer working with Peter.

'You were a ward sister before coming here, weren't you?' Gemma was asking, pouring more coffee for them both, as Laura just caught a glimpse of the tall, slim figure of Peter, in white coat, chatting away to Joan Barnard. 'Laura, do you feel all right?'

'Er. . .yes, thanks, fine. What was it you said just now?'

Gemma groaned, repeating the original question.

'Yes, I was ward sister for a short while. I enjoyed it.'

'We could put in for it, I suppose.'

'I'll have a think,' Laura said non-committally, wanting to change the subject. 'How's Ken, by the way? Have you heard from him since he left for New York?'

'No, but I did make that phone call before he went —you know, the one we discussed, about us both feeling the same. I think it worked.' Gemma smiled, her eyes, instead of Laura's, taking on a rather far-away look now. 'As soon as I told him what I felt and more about plans for the wedding, he cheered up quite a lot.'

'So he wasn't grouching any more about you being up here?'

'Thank heaven, no. In fact he actually said as we're both working away we can save more, and once he's back home he might even fancy transferring to the service up here, then I could work at the Lodge as a non-resident.'

'Sounds terrific, Gemma! It'll all work out now, you'll see!'

Back on the ward, Laura went straight to little Tiki. Despite all they had done, the disease seemed to be taking a firm hold. His breathing was noisy, the dry cough more troublesome, and while doing what she could to make the little one's breathing easier Peter arrived, saying, 'There's real difficulty with that breathing now, I'm afraid. We may have to do a tracheostomy to relieve the laryngeal obstruction.'

'Poor little soul,' Laura murmured. 'You don't think it could just be a foreign body in the air passages, apart from confirmation of the disease, I mean?'

'No, I examined him thoroughly when I came in last night for that very reason, but no go, I'm afraid.'

Laura did the round of the rest of the patients with Peter, their last call being on Yasmin. She was lying in her bed and, as they walked in, stuffed something under her pillow. Peter greeted her as usual, then spoke slowly and carefully in English, again surprised at the way this sixteen-year-old had absorbed so much. 'You will be getting up this afternoon, Yasmin?' He smiled at her warmly.

The girl nodded, although her face looked sad. 'I will. I had a dream last night. . .of Nadja. . . It made me cry. . .I keep her letter under my pillow.'

Laura took the girl's hand. 'We understand, dear. She is thinking of you too, you know.'

Peter, meanwhile, was examining some red spots on Yasmin's arms. 'Oh, Lord, this could be scabies. Thank heaven she hasn't been in contact with the rest.' He turned back the bedcovers and inspected her long, thin legs, her trunk and groin. In her own language he asked if the spots troubled her now that a rash was breaking out. She said they itched a little. With a sympathetic smile he reverted to English. 'Do not worry, Yasmin, we'll soon get rid of it.'

'Can I not now get up?'

'Yes, but you must stay in your room for a while, I'm afraid, away from everyone else.'

As they walked back to the office, having scrubbed up at the basin in Yasmin's room, Peter instructed Laura to do all that was necessary to combat the skin disease. 'A hot bath first, of the whole body, application of benzyl benzoate—twenty-five per cent—over the entire body, and a repeat bath after twenty-four hours. Fingers crossed it's not going to lead to impetigo.

'This is the trouble; we have no idea who these people have been in contact with, and it seems these diseases break out once they've had decent care and food, and relaxed mentally, poor little devils.

'Don't forget also, Laura, stress daily washing of all

parts of the body. All her present clothing and bedding must be fumigated and sterilised; bedlinen must be changed daily. And if anyone recalls seeing Yasmin in contact with any of the other patients it must be the same treatment for them.'

'Well, as far as I know she has preferred to be on her own since Nadja's death, so we might just avoid an outbreak.'

He said quickly, 'I'll inform the cross-infection committee straight away; that's the second outbreak this week, including the diphtheria. We'll have to review the amount of cross-infection occurring and what steps should be taken to control it.'

He headed for the office door, the rather irrelevant thought striking him that the lilac colour of Laura's uniform dress made her eyes look deep violet, and he said suddenly, 'By the way, there's an engagement party we're invited to tonight, those who can be spared. It's very short notice, but it's one of our registrars, who's due to go off on a six-month course tomorrow. His fiancée, who has only just qualified at Aberdeen as a junior doctor, is going with him before she finds a suitable post, somewhere up here, hopefully.'

He smiled.

'That's nice; I heard about the romance, actually. A love at first sight thing, I believe,' she said, eyes bright.

'It happens!' he grinned, then popped his head back round the door. 'You didn't say if you're able to come or not?'

'Everything's looking good for it!' she called, trying not to feel too pleased that he had seemed quite keen on her going. Then her spirits plummeted again as she recorded Tiki's infection in the sepsis book. She was stringing too many possibilities together with this man. Friendship could be a fine thing between two people. Why on earth couldn't her thoughts stop there? Instead of which, even hearing of the soon-to-be-engaged couple made her suddenly have a madly untamed day-dream of Peter and herself heading for the same blissful situation.

She added Yasmin's name in the book beneath Tiki's, then closed it with a sigh. She was darned if she'd allow Peter Wentworth to disturb her peace of mind; she loved her work too much. It was crazy; surely there were other quite eligible men in the build-ing who perhaps wouldn't play havoc with her heart so much?

That evening Laura dressed carefully. The party was at nine, so there was just about time to shower and change. Standing before her full-length mirror, she smoothed down the soft folds of her calf-length, peach silk dress, with its small fitted waist and strapless top, and gave a small frown, not able to decide if the gold necklace and earrings her parents had given her, were too much. But she decided that with her hair worn in a loose pageboy style to her shoulders it would probably be OK.

She put the finishing touches to her make-up and sprayed on a flowery perfume—which she remembered she had done once already—then slipped into high-heeled sandals. Picking up her small handbag with its gold shoulder chain, which would at least allow her to balance a glass and a plate in the scrum that usually developed on these occasions, she was ready.

She knew she was fussing. The possibility of seeing Peter at a social event, with everyone dressing up for it, had panicked her, which was quite mad. To be sophisticated like him would be far more to the point. But, however attractive she might look, nothing could stop the frantic fluttering of her heart as she considered the mind-blowing possibility of dancing in close proximity with him—or even just talking to him, watching the way his mouth tilted slightly to one side when he was thinking, the cleft that appeared by the corner of his mouth with startling suddenness. . .

Giving an impatient groan at her own weak will, she checked she had her room key and went downstairs to the sports club where the party was in full swing. It was very festive—quite amazing what a group of people, including some of the new musical club, could do in a few hours. Dennis was excelling himself on the keyboard, his faithful friend on the drums, and someone she didn't know was doing a good job with an electric guitar.

'Hi, Laura!' Gemma came rushing up to her. 'I'm so glad you're here—I don't know half these people!'

'Come on, girls, what are you having to drink?' The host and his new fiancée were welcoming them, and the party was well underway as the crowd swelled. Laura even caught a brief glimpse of Joan Barnard, looking most attractive dancing with Mr Lomax.

'Laura. . .!' Peter was smiling at her, elegantly casual in a dark suit, as most of the men seemed to be wearing. Later, when jackets were discarded, they would look more like their usual selves. 'Great to see you! Let's test the floor, shall we?'

Taken by surprise, Laura had little time to recall all the pitfalls she'd been dreading, especially when she heard Peter saying, 'You look terrific. I can scarcely believe my eyes, when I saw you at work only an hour ago!'

'A little less, I think! We girls have to work fast, you know!'

While dancing with Tim Hudson later, Laura tried hard to concentrate on what he was saying, while being so aware of Peter, wherever he happened to be on the floor, dancing with some of the staff. Just at that moment he and his partner drew level with herself and Tim, calling, 'Another two minutes and it's time for my speech of congratulations, Tim; don't forget to come and give me some support!'

'Don't worry, Pete, there's half a dozen of us about to do that!'

The speech was short, witty and to the point. The happy couple were thrilled with their combined present, given to them by Miss Menzies, who, it was noticed, was accompanied by a tall, distinguished-looking man whom nobody knew. When the music struck up again, Dennis had swapped with another musician to claim Laura for a dance. His round, good-natured face was wreathed in smiles. 'You look smashing tonight, Laura, if I may say so!'

'Thanks, Dennis! You look jolly good yourself!'

'You're a little tease, that's what you are!'

'No, I really meant it, honestly—' The pop group suddenly stopped, silence was demanded and an announcement made.

'Emergency, folks! Will Mr Peter Wentworth go immediately to Primrose ward, please? Staff Nurse Meadows also. There may be two more of the specialist team needed later, but we'll leave that for the doc to decide.'

Back on Primrose, Laura hurriedly cast off her dress in the staff cloakroom and put on a fresh uniform available for such emergencies. She met Peter in the corridor. 'It's Tiki,' he said quickly. 'I've just had them prepare Theatre. He's cyanosed and I'll have to do a tracheostomy. I've told Theatre Sister you'll be assisting.'

Laura and Night Sister prepared Tiki on the ward. His skin was bluish, the strident rasp of his breathing pitiful to hear. 'The oxygen's helping a little now,' the woman on the other side of the cot whispered worriedly. 'Is Mr Wentworth ready in Theatre, Staff?'

'Yes, he was on his way there when I came in. If we give Tiki the pre-med now we can get him there immediately.'

Between them they took the sick baby on a trolley, his life seeming to be ebbing away before their eyes. Once in Theatre, staff were suitably garbed in their sterile clothing. The anaesthetist checked that Tiki had lost consciousness, then gave a thumbs-up sign to Peter. The operation would not take long, but hopefully would be life-saving. Laura watched Peter make a deft incision in the trachea below the cricoid cartilage. A tracheostomy tube was inserted and kept clear of mucus by drawing it out with a fine rubber tube attached to a suction apparatus.

Above his mask Peter glanced at the equipment. 'Thank God for a powerful electric one. At last,' he murmured quietly, doing a final check, 'I think that's it, for now. If the breathing doesn't improve after this, we'll have to assist him by connecting the tracheostomy tube to the electronically controlled respirator, so rhythmically inflating the lungs. Now, we can only wait and see.' He glanced up at the wall clock. 'There's not a lot more we can do at present, Sister. Do you think Staff and I might go back to the dance?' he said, with a bewitching grin.

Theatre Sister responded, as he knew she would, 'I see no reason why not, sir. You've done all that's possible. I dare say you'll have quite a bit to do tomorrow—' she grinned knowingly '—so enjoy yourself; make hay and all that! I'll contact you if there's any change.'

'You're a little gem, Sister, do you know that?'

'Flatterer!' she said soberly, but looking pleased.

*   *   *

An hour later Laura and Peter were entering with gusto into the Gay Gordons, which someone had clamoured for because, as a non-Scot, he wanted to show off; that was what Peter said anyway, as they swept across the floor in formation. '*You're* quite good at this, Laura; it's years since I've indulged. My mother used to despair of me ever learning to dance as a callow youth!'

Too soon came the final dance of the evening. Laura had had several partners but when Peter sought her out for this particular one a rush of sweet joy went through her. She had tried hard not to expect any of her wishes about the dance to come true, but now the lights were low; dreamy music washed over them as he held her close. Romance was in the air, the happiness of the newly engaged couple palpable, as if bringing a tide of harmony and sentiment with it.

Peter's strong, smooth cheek was pressed against hers, their steps in harmony, seeming to blend perfectly; in fact her entire body seemed to be in tune with his. It was sheer heaven dancing with him—as she'd always imagined. She knew she was allowing herself to fall into this delicious state of submission but cared nothing at that moment for the rest of the world.

'Penny for them,' he murmured softly in her ear, his lips brushing the lobe, making a shudder of desire go through her.

'Secrets. . .' she whispered back.

'Tell me, then, if you've enjoyed yourself tonight, apart, that is, from the work-break!'

'It's been far better than I thought, thinking of work. I imagined Tiki would remain on my mind. . .' She looked at him seriously for a moment. 'Is it too selfish of me to be having such a happy evening when that poor little one is so sick?'

He shook his head, smiling down at her, dark eyes

understanding, mouth tilted thoughtfully. 'My dear Laura, we're not expected to take on all the troubles in the world, which we do anyway. But tonight is one of those occasions when we're both going to close the door on them and be most horribly selfish. . .just for a while. . .'

CHAPTER SEVEN

IT WAS a serenely lovely evening when Peter and Laura left the party after taking their leave of everyone, the air sweet and scented after the heat of the sports club. Peter said suddenly, 'Supposing you slip indoors for some sensible shoes, Laura, and we'll walk beside the loch for a while? I'll wait outside the entrance here.'

'OK, I'll only be a minute.' Her feet sped up the stairs to her room. She put on her flat shoes and hurried down again, not wanting to lose a moment of this perfect evening. Surely it was all too good to be true? she told herself as Peter took her arm and they strolled together on the narrow sandy shore of the loch. The moon's rim was just appearing over the darkened silhouette of the hills. Stars shone with a diamond brightness, and their reflection in the water was like a sea of jewels. They stopped to admire the scene in front of them.

'It's fantastic,' Laura murmured, so conscious of Peter's presence at her side. She didn't move; didn't turn her head. She sensed he was looking down at her, perhaps his own thoughts with the girl he had loved and lost, of what might have been. Laura knew now the meaning of 'sweet sorrow', yet for her there was no parting because in a sense there had been no beginning, and yet at this very moment, amid such mind-wrenching beauty, how could she help but feel a deep affinity for this man who had attracted her from the very first day she had met him?

A faint movement at her side made her heart race as his hand touched hers; gently, tenderly, he drew her round to face him, cupping her cheeks in his hands, gazing at her, whispering, 'I can't stop myself from telling you how enchanting you look tonight, Laura. It was sheer torture when I wasn't dancing with you, do you know that?' His hands dropped to her shoulders, smooth as alabaster in the moonlight. His half-smile, the one she knew so well, was in his eyes as they held hers. 'I can see by your expression what you're thinking,' he said.

'I'd like to hear it.' She smiled up at him.

'You're thinking that you've heard all this before, and I've said it to other girls more than once. Am I right?'

'Something like that.'

'But you're wrong, Laura; as far as I'm concerned there's a friendship between us that's unique and can never change. I'm sure that's how it is for you. . .' He lowered his head slowly, his lips so close to hers that she almost stopped breathing as contact was made and the world spun madly, madly out of control. He had not drawn her closer to him but held her hands while they moved slightly apart, his expression difficult to define as he said, as if perhaps half expecting her to resist him, 'Also, Laura, there's an attraction I feel so strongly between us that is far removed from friendship. It's as if our meeting was meant to be; I really mean that.'

She tried to fend off the sense of the right chemistry she felt they had between them as she said softly, 'Peter, please don't think I'm expecting you to say such things just because. . .because its a romantic interlude on this particular night. Besides, you still have your memories of Marika. I do understand, you know.'

Briefly his eyes strayed across the gleaming water, then back to her; he said nothing, just encircled her with his arms, the pounding of his heartbeat against hers like a primeval message between them. She was drowning; her legs were weak; had he not held her she would have slipped down to the ground.

All consideration for Marika suddenly went as she heard his low groan of desire; their kisses burned and passion seared between them, their bodies tortured with longing. The tall, agile figure in her arms, whose every muscle, every sinew seemed attuned to hers, was the man who had stepped straight from her dreams.

'Laura, my darling,' he was murmuring. 'I appreciate everything you say, but life sweeps us along with it at times. Marika and I lived and loved in an entirely different world. Now the world is new again, we all have another chance to start afresh, and one thing I am absolutely sure of is that, in whatever guise or form, love will always be "the ruling passion".'

Gently he tilted her chin, brushed her lips lightly with his, saying in a low undertone, 'Come back with me to the flat—please, Laura; there are so many things I want to say to you.' God! His heart was already ruling his head. . .

That was the moment when she could have said no, but instead she said nothing, just returned the pressure of his hand as he took hers and together they walked, words an unnecessary intervention. All around them the dark velvety night and the sense of nature's organised plan for man, bird and beast was very potent—especially when quite suddenly, with a swift, silent movement, a small herd of deer appeared through the trees and emerged on to the path, their antlers impressive. Peter whispered quickly, 'Don't move; we'll scare them away; one of the bucks is selecting a mate.'

Two majestically built bucks began skirmishing between themselves, a female hind the object of their desire, antlers clashing amid much snorting until the

losing buck was chased off and the young hind sniffed
and inspected the buck. They ducked heads together
and, giving a strangely cough-like grunt in the final
assesment, playfully touched heads, performing a love-
ritual by contact. With the decision made, the two
leapt away in chase, disappearing into the thick pines as
silently as they had come, the rest of the herd scattering
deeper into the woods.

'I've never seen anything like it,' Laura whispered
in awestruck tones.

Peter smiled. 'Certainly not something one would
see in the daytime, with other people around.'

His hand tightened upon hers as they walked on, the
scene one that would remain in Laura's mind forever.

In the comfortable sitting-room of Peter's three-
roomed flat he took her coat, removing his own jacket
before pouring drinks for them both. She hadn't sat
down, but watched him in the tiny kitchen busying
himself with bottles and glasses. He put his arm around
her as they sat on the large settee together, and he
raised his glass to her. 'Thank you, Laura, for a perfect
evening.' His eyes admired the smooth, peach-like
beauty of her bare shoulders, the delectable cleavage
between her full and rounded breasts. He was a fool,
he thought, to be lured this way. Wasn't it only creating
further complications? And yet. . .

As his eyes burned into hers, Laura knew her own
were returning the admiration deeply reflected in his.
She sipped the whisky they had decided upon, saying
in response to his words, 'It has been unforgettable.'

'There was so much I wanted to say, Laura,' he
murmured hoarsely, warmth spreading through him
where their thighs touched, 'and yet I can think of
none of it at this particular moment; you're mesmeris-
ing me. . .' He lifted her free hand to his lips, kissing
the tip of each finger, the tide of passion running high.

She traced a hand over the firm line of his jaw, the smooth dark brows, hairline, forehead, the lobes of his ears, until he almost snatched the glass from her, putting it aside, then claiming her lips, tongues touching, all constraint banished. They were of one mind, and the dizzy heights reached out to them, from which there was no return. . .

Peter lowered his head to kiss the breasts that had been longing for his touch. 'My God, Laura, you're truly the temptress I've always dreamed about.' He took her hands, drawing her willingly to another room. His bed, king-size with a satin quilt, was soft and yielding. With quiet savagery he stripped the satin and lace from her skin. She unbuttoned his shirt with studied slowness, kissing the broad chest with its newly healed scar, then released his torso from the rest of his clothes.

His kisses were ranging over her body in a shower of adoration, making her cry out for more as their bodies met in recognition of each other's perfection. The world they entered was one of dazzling lights, sensuous plateaus and whirling impressions, like a fiery Catherine wheel that spun in utter sensuality and complete surrender, before burning itself out. . .

Only after coming back to earth and lying sated in each other's arms did the first joy, followed by sadness, return to Laura. . .

Peter leaned up on his elbow, brushing back the soft, shining hair, seeing the faint mist of tears in those sultry violet eyes. 'Please, Laura, don't be upset. I know perhaps it shouldn't have happened, but it was inevitable, my darling. Selfishly I wanted the evening to go this way, especially when I saw you looking so ravishing tonight. I know that sounds disgracefully macho, but that's not quite how I meant it. My thoughts are still reeling at the moment; we'll talk later when we're back on terra firma!'

She stroked his cheek. 'I'm not really upset, Peter, but I do feel I should have put up some kind of opposition! Still,' she said hurriedly, 'we'll forget the whole thing. . .'

She knew she couldn't possibly do that, but somehow had to let him think she had no claim upon him, either mentally or physically. 'I must get back to my own bed now.' She smiled sleepily. 'Thank heaven we know we'll not be the only ones looking hung over in the morning!'

'That's for sure! I'll make us some coffee first then walk you back.'

Next morning Laura went immediately to Tiki's room. A tent had been erected over him to prevent draughts. The night sister appeared, taking an anxious look at him. 'I'm glad to say he's stable,' she said in answer to Laura's question. 'Mr Wentworth came in at dawn this morning.'

'What about Tiki's breathing?'

'Easier, comparatively.'

Just then Peter joined them. 'Good morning,' he said brusquely, examining the tracheostomy site. 'Since Tiki's inhaled air is no longer warmed and moistened by passage through the nose and pharynx,' he went on, as they all moved away from the child's hearing for fear of anything that might revive a cough and dislodge the tube, 'I want him to have a steam kettle to moisten the air; that'll make him a lot more comfortable.' He said to Laura, 'Perhaps you'd take the night report; I'm sure Sister wants to get off to bed.'

Laura had just discussed Tiki with Miss Menzies when Peter returned; his eyes meeting hers, he said in a businesslike fashion, 'I want young Yasmin to get up now for a few hours each day; she must remain isolated in her room, but I want to encourage her to entertain herself—looking at books, listening to music, drawing, painting—anything to prevent her dwelling upon Nadja. Later we may have to be quite firm with her.'

'I agree,' Laura said thoughtfully.

'Also, Hyacinth must now be made available for the six patients on their way here from Croatia. There's little need to wait for the selection process; they're all wounded and needing surgery, I'm told.' He added, with a wry grin, 'So make the most of the lull at present!'

'I'll do that little thing!'

He turned at the door. 'Miss Menzies told me at breakfast you may be considering the application for promotion. Are you sure that's what you want, Laura?'

He spoke her name like a caress and she knew what he meant; his thoughts had run along the same lines as hers. Quickly she glanced away from the expression in his eyes. 'I didn't want to, Peter—in fact had decided not to. But after last—but on due consideration,' she stumbled, 'I thought it best. . .'

'But I don't want you to leave the team, Laura. You must know that. We work well together, always have. Change your mind, *please*.'

She couldn't resist his plea. Neither did she want to. 'Very well, just for now, perhaps.'

His relieved smile brought the joy flooding back as he said, 'I'll explain to Miss Menzies that I need you.'

And, with those words ringing like bells in her ears all day, she carried on with her work.

That evening Peter sought her out in the staff common-room, fetching tea for them both and sitting alongside her. 'It's great news that Tiki's still making small improvements; his fever's almost down to normal now, I see.'

'Yes, he's such a good little chap when we change his dressing; twice a day is no fun for him, but his large, intelligent eyes seem to be getting more alert by the minute.'

Peter was sipping his tea thoughtfully. 'I happened to be glancing through the Inverness newspaper this morning. At last they're advertising the visit of a concert pianist giving a recital there. I don't know her, but it sounds OK. Will you come?'

'Thanks. Love to.'

'Terrific. Talking about music, there's a rehearsal for us tomorrow, ready for Saturday. Don't forget; we hope to have our first real audience from the Lodge.'

'Heck! I think I'll develop a headache!'

'Don't you dare! I'm looking forward to hearing you play again.'

She glanced down at her fingers, conscious of the way he was looking at her. 'Peter,' she murmured breathlessly, glad that the common-room had emptied, 'about last night. . .'

He placed a finger against her lips. 'Please, no. . .'

She respected his wish, saying quickly, 'OK. Afraid I must go now; I'm on until eight tonight. Bye now.'

The rehearsal was very good the following evening. Gemma surpassed herself and suggested to Laura that together they play some of the more popular pieces of light music. The musical combination produced by the two girls seemed to create an atmosphere that fell lyrically upon the ears of the other musicians, especially when they played their own arrangement of Robert Burns' 'A Red, Red Rose'.

Laura knew that Peter was watching her as she sat easily at the piano, her slim fingers running over the keys, Burns' poetic images reminding her of her own night of love that would live forever in her heart as a

song that was never-ending. . . Quickly she shook herself from the reverie she had fallen into, especially
when Peter strode across the room to the small dais.
Amid the spontaneous applause he smiled. 'Well done,
girls; you're going to be one of our star turns
tomorrow, I can see that!'

Gemma chuckled. 'We thought we'd go for a swim,
didn't we, Laura?'

Dennis overheard the remark. 'If you do, I'll come
and fish you out, bikinis and all, then you'll have to
play like that!'

'Dennis! You are dreadful!' Gemma teased, to a
background of cheers from the rest.

The following night was a quite amazing success.
Afterwards Peter and Laura drove to the village for a
drink in the cosy, friendly atmosphere of the inn that
had become 'theirs', as Peter put it. 'I've sent for the
tickets for Inverness, Laura, so mark it in your diary.
Can you manage to wangle the afternoon off as well
as the evening?'

'Great! I'm sure I can. By the way, Miss Menzies
was telling us about the expected admissions. She's
recruited four more nurses to "float" for a while until
we see where they're best needed.'

They talked on companionably, Peter suddenly saying, 'Did I tell you I'm organising a more formal
English class shortly? Those people due to arrive, most
of whom can't speak our language, can be included.
I'm thinking of taking two groups, both young and
adult, hopefully.'

Seeing the enthusiasm on his face, Laura said with
a grin, 'You are a nice man, Peter. I think Miss
Menzies is quite lucky to have you here.'

'Heavens! There's nothing special about me; I'm the
one who's lucky to be here.' He smiled, bringing the
cleft in view. 'And, had it not been for a certain staff

nurse of my acquaintance, I might not be sitting here now!'

She smiled at the recollection. 'Strange, wasn't it? That afternoon, the first thing I noticed was how tired you looked. The others were, of course, but I just had this sixth sense that something was about to happen!'

He was chuckling. 'So you'd polished up the old crystal ball even then!'

They walked back to the car, Peter turning to look at her before switching on the ignition. 'You know, Laura, tonight, listening to you play, made me realise the intense joy you're able to give to people.' She felt his hand upon hers, the firm, steady grip, the warmth, as if he wanted to communicate but had his own reasons for holding back the words. Even as they set off her hand was still in his. 'Not strictly legal,' he laughed, 'but let's hope only the deer will notice.'

His mentioning those beautiful creatures as they rode beside the loch brought a fresh reminder of their recent lovemaking. There was an easy silence between the two of them and Laura was convinced that, at times, all he had gone through abroad rose up to confront him, overwhelming everything else—something she was learning to understand.

With the imminent intake of the new patients in the following week, the days were busy ones for Laura. Baby Tiki was making slow if steady progress since his operation. A tracheostomy tube with two inner tubes was in use, one having an expiratory tube to allow the baby to swallow, and hopefully to begin making the sort of infant noises that babies indulged in. Shortly they hoped to start feeding him with an adequate fluid diet by spoon rather than the artificial means now employed.

One morning Laura bathed and changed André in

the so-called baby-room, where everything was set out for easy use. He was gurgling happily at her as she placed him gently on the scales. 'You sweet thing,' she cooed, 'you think its your playtime, don't you? Well, it's not mine, darling.' She laughed, picking him up for his usual cuddle after recording his regular weight gain. It was weekly now instead of daily. 'Soon, when the sunshine's warmer, we're going to put you outside, then you can watch all the birds flying about, and one day you'll tell me all about it. . .in English!'

Giving him a gentle kiss on the top of his dark, silky curls, she placed him back in his cot, noticing a new rattle she hadn't seen before. 'Well, that's nice,' she grinned. 'Another pressie, I see! Someone else has been spoiling you again, haven't they?' she said, handing him the colourful toy.

Pearl appeared at her side, admiring him too. 'Isn't he gorgeous? Hello, you little poppet, you love your aunty Pearly, don't you, sweetheart?'

'It wouldn't be Aunty Pearly who has just bought him yet another new rattle, would it?' Laura asked wickedly.

'Not me at this time of the month,' Pearl laughed. 'I guess it was Mr Wentworth; I thought I saw him at André's cotside yesterday afternoon, and he came away looking quite pleased with himself.

'Still, he's not the only one. Dennis is quite a big softie with him too, you know. Did I tell you he bought André a woolly white lamb? Of course, André was *sucking* it! I had to retrieve it and tell Dennis very diplomatically that it was not the best of things for children of André's age. Men are weird creatures, aren't they?' She chuckled, and walked off to answer the phone, calling, 'Course, they haven't got brains like us.'

She was back in seconds. 'Talk of the devil, Mr

Wentworth wants a word with you, Laura.'

'OK, thanks.' She reached for the phone.

'Staff Nurse Meadows.'

'Ah, Laura.' The voice came over with its usual power to make her heart spin on its axis. 'I've just had a word with Miss Menzies about the sister promotion stakes. She fully understands that I want to retain you in the team, so that's all fixed up.'

'Oh, thanks, Peter.'

'I have to go to a meeting in a short while, Laura, so I won't be doing the round. Mr Lomax is on call if you want him. How is young Tiki this morning?'

'He had four hours' sleep non-stop last night, so he's keeping up the progress.'

'Thank goodness for that. Have you managed to get tomorrow organised for Inverness?'

'Yes, I'm finishing at twelve.'

'Excellent. I thought we'd have lunch at Brora on the way through, then there'll be time for dinner at Inverness.'

'I'm looking forward to it immensely, Peter.'

'Me too. I'll pick you up tomorrow midday.'

Laura replaced the receiver slowly, if only to get herself together. She really had to stop this complete immersion of every other thought to the exclusion of all else when Peter spoke to her. When they were working together it was no problem, but during casual conversation and at social events just happy, chatty conversation seemed to change her, as if he were the eighth wonder of the world. . .

With a small shake of her head, she went back to see if two-year-old Marie was still sleeping. She was, and cuddling her old toy duck. Unfortunately they had begun to suspect that she was showing signs of a heart disorder. Because of it, a friend of Peter's, an eminent heart man, was coming from Edinburgh to see the child and give his prognosis in four days' time.

She swept the dark hair from the little girl's face.
She did not wake, but in her sleep clutched the duck
more tightly, as if her subconscious was warning that
she might lose her most precious possession. Laura
turned away with a sigh. Poor little soul, she'd had a
miserable start to her life, and seemingly for the rest
of her formative years would be cared for by one
person after another. Why, she wondered, should these
children have to suffer because of man's greed and his
lust for war?

Saturday morning dawned bright and clear; even dry.
By midday Laura was practically ready to meet Peter.
She had given up her coffee-break time, using it to
slip away to get changed, as staff often did. Now,
glancing at her cherry-red suit and black polo-necked
sweater, she hoped the outfit would carry her through
the events of the day. She threw a warm white coat
over her arm and tucked a silk scarf into her shoulder-
bag, at the last minute remembered a quick spray of
perfume, and was ready.

She sped down the stairs, and saw the BMW already
waiting. Her heart turned over as Peter got out of the
car and came to meet her.

'Hi, Laura! Hope it wasn't too much of a rush?'

'No,' she laughed as they settled into the luxurious
upholstery. 'Once or twice time positively dragged!'

'I know the feeling!' he said as they moved off.
'Well, I must say I'm longing to see this Rosamund
Hedley. I've been so long away from civilisation, and
one quickly loses touch. I believe this woman is of
international fame and a world concert pianist. Apparently her concerts are a sell-out.'

'Yes, I have to confess myself I'm not very well up
on the giants of the music world at the moment. It's

an ever changing process anyway, don't you think?'

'Indeed, art is a living thing and thank heaven for it.'

They lunched at Brora, the meal excellently served with a leisurely air that enabled them to sit talking between courses, taking their time, conversation ranging from the serious to the jocular. Over coffee, Peter said suddenly, 'I love the way we can communicate with each other so easily and naturally, Laura. I feel that neither of us would be even mildly shocked at what the other said, whatever it was.'

Her heart sang at the compliment. 'I feel exactly the same. It's strange, isn't it, that advantage doesn't necessarily come with friendship? I had a boyfriend before I came up here and I realise now there's a point where couples meet a barrier, and the easy atmosphere between them suddenly comes to a full stop, usually because of a misunderstanding over something quite trivial. That's what I found with this particular friend, anyway.'

'Then the affair ended, presumably?'

'Definitely. There's occasionally that lucky situation where one knows it's right from the very beginning, but one has to learn these things.'

'How true. . .'

As they left the hotel a weak sun shone behind shower-filled clouds. As they carried on with the journey there was a closeness of feeling between them which, Laura decided, must be the ultimate in happiness. Halfway they stopped for tea at a small, white-washed house that had a walled garden full of hyacinths and when the sun broke through the perfume was unforgettable.

Finally they arrived at Inverness, the waters of the Moray Firth brilliant in the afternoon light, the royal burgh, on record from the late twelfth century, founded by David I, still retaining its role as a market town and administrative centre, giving it prominence to the present day. They saw the oldest surviving houses, one a typical sixteenth century type with slate roof and crow-stepped gables, its interior now modern offices. Laura noticed with interest a marriage lintel dated 1681 over the fireplace.

Peter said laughingly, as they carried on out to Church Street, which was one of the oldest streets in the burgh, and the notable Dunbar's Hospital, 'Oh, if only we had more time.'

They had dinner at a restaurant near the Town Steeple, still chatting about the surrounding history. Peter was looking at her as she sat back, replete. 'That was a lovely meal, Peter. It's been such a good day.'

He grinned. 'Your presence would gladden any man's heart,' he told her sincerely, thinking how charmingly easy she was to be with.

On their way to the concert hall large coin spots of rain began to fall. They joined the queue, then, with suppressed excitement, were shown to their seats. Peter presented her with a box of chocolates and a programme, after which they settled down with breathless anticipation of the evening before them. Peter helped her slip off her coat, then took her hand in his, the contact like an electric shock to Laura, the feeling so intense. . .so right.

Then the lights lowered, the scarlet curtains slid back, and just briefly they glanced into each other's eyes, words unnecessary, especially when the full orchestra rose as one in deference to the famous artist when she appeared.

She was beautiful, tall, slender, with dark, shining hair dressed in an elaborately upswept coiffure. Bowing elegantly, she took her place at the grand piano, a hush falling over the audience as the conductor raised his baton. The first piece was Bach's Adagio from

Prelude No. 4, a great favourite of Laura's. Peter's hand had tightened upon hers, and she had never felt so blissfully happy in her whole life. With the first lilting piano chords, they leaned forward together to get a closer glimpse of this celebrated exponent of the magic they were now listening to.

Then Peter's hand tensed, allowing hers to fall from his grasp, and he leaned forward more rigidly, a frown between his eyes. A cold fear gripped Laura as he muttered, so that Laura could barely discern the words, 'My God, I know her! But I had no idea of her stage name.' He slumped back into his seat as if shocked to the core, running a hand over his face.

'Peter, are you all right?' Laura whispered anxiously. 'Shall we go outside where it's cooler?'

He shook his head, looking at her in a daze. 'No. . . no,' he muttered. ''I'll be OK. . .'

She left him to himself, apparently deep in a world of his own. She was devastated. She no longer heard any of the music, which now seemed just an intrusive cacophony of sound. Peter sat as if carved in stone. During the interlude, he insisted that he did not want to leave, but they went to the bar together and had a cool drink. He said little that threw any light upon the matter. Laura tried to draw him out about Rosamund Hedley, but all he would say was that he had once known her, and it was a bad shock seeing her so unexpectedly.

Laura knew now that the spell of the evening had vanished and all she wanted was to head for the Lodge. 'Shall we go back?' she said with feeling. 'I really don't mind, you know.'

He shook his head. 'No, we must stay until the end. Forgive me; this is the very last thing I expected.'

They returned for the second half of the concert, but Peter was exactly the same; it was as if the man she knew had gone away. The journey home was difficult, to say the least. Once in the car, he said suddenly, 'You may have to drive if necessary, Laura; a wretched migraine's coming on, I think.'

'That's OK; just tell me when you want to swap.'

But the miles sped by and he continued driving. Laura suspected a migraine was some way from the truth. The evening had ended very differently from how she had imagined, and it seemed that once again his past was catching up on him. On arrival at the Lodge there were no kisses, no embraces that had filled her once before with wild hopes and longings, just a brief goodnight between them.

'I'm deeply sorry about this, Laura, believe me. I wouldn't have gone if I'd known this was going to happen. Perhaps later, but not now, I'll explain. You've been so understanding; I can't tell you how much I appreciate it.'

'That's OK, Peter,' she said evenly. 'I do hope you feel better tomorrow.' She lifted her chin in bravado, giving a polite little smile, but felt wretched as she left him at the entrance to her building. Once inside she did not allow any tears, but decided to put the entire incident down to experience. Common sense simply had to take over. After all, Peter had suffered a great deal and no doubt the majestic sweep of the music, along with a sighting of someone who reminded him of the past, had tugged hard at his emotions.

Wasn't this also another pointer to herself that she must withhold her own feelings from now on? After all, this man's attractions had so swiftly overwhelmed her, but his sudden change of attitude tonight surely had to act as a warning?

CHAPTER EIGHT

FORTUNATELY next day no one asked Laura if she had enjoyed the trip. She preferred to keep the entire thing to herself. Had anyone seen Peter give her a lift the day before it was a perfectly normal thing to do at the Lodge. Nevertheless, the whole event had wrought such havoc upon her mind that over lunch she was driven to speak to Gemma.

'Do you mind if we have coffee in my room? It's about Peter Wentworth.'

Upstairs, Laura outlined the trip to Inverness, leaving aside the emotional content. Even so, Gemma, realising at last that she herself was in love, could spot the signs in others. 'You haven't fallen for the guy, have you?'

Laura didn't deny or confirm it. 'I just don't know, Gem. At this moment I know nothing.' She ran a hand across her distraught face. 'We were having a super day. It all seemed so right until the awful moment when he saw Rosamund Hedley. Her presence seemed to snuff the real Peter Wentworth out of all recognition.'

'I don't quite understand, Laura,' Gemma said, frowning.

'Well, I believe the person on stage was someone he'd been involved with—maybe still is, for all I know. It shook him terribly. He told me once that he'd had a girlfriend in the Red Cross who was killed, but who this one is it's impossible to say. All I know is that she had one hell of an effect upon him.'

Gemma said slowly, 'Well, quite honestly, I don't think there's a lot you can do but sort of keep your distance for a while. Be your normal self, don't ask anything about his private life, appear not to give a damn. I would! Don't forget if you hadn't gone to the concert with him this would never have come about.'

Laura nodded, not too sure that she entirely agreed with Gemma. 'You could be right, Gem, but it's been good to talk it over with you; the whole thing had begun to get quite out of hand in my mind. Keep it to yourself, though; I don't want him to think I'm going around broadcasting his business.'

Gemma put a friendly arm around Laura's shoulders as they went downstairs. 'It's all between you and me, love. I was glad of your help with Ken and me.'

Later the two girls were at one of Miss Menzies' meetings with the staff. They had covered a lot of ground when she said suddenly, 'Mr Wentworth will be performing several ops in the coming two or three days; should any nurses wish to observe these through the viewing panel, please contact Theatre Sister.'

She gave them a big smile: 'Well, now for some good news that indirectly will affect us all. The Press, both local and national, have been in touch with me. As you may or may not know, the famous pianist, Rosamund Hedley, has been giving sell-out performances in Inverness this week; some of you may have already been to see her. Miss Hedley has heard—no doubt the Press also—that sick and wounded children, perhaps from her own country of Bosnia, are being cared for at the Lodge, and she has announced her intention to give an extra charity concert for them. She has sent us a few complimentary tickets and anyone who has time off, would they see me and I'll hand them out? Should there not be enough to go round I'm assured that—according to Miss Hedley—a word in her agent's ear will sort that out.'

She glanced at the time. 'The only snag being that

the concert is scheduled for tomorrow, so it means fast decisions.'

Gemma and Laura walked back to Primrose, both thoughtful. In the lift Gemma said, 'Well, it looks as if this lovely lady has a big heart, I'll say that for her.'

Laura spent the rest of the day in a sombre mood. The only good thing about it was that Tiki's tube had been removed and the incision closed. They hoped he would be completely recovered in a few weeks' time; nevertheless, treatment had to be continued until three consecutive throat swabs showed negative for diphtheria bacilli.

She had not seen Peter, but knew he was on duty. By afternoon she wondered if she should ring to ask how the migraine was, but discarded the idea. It was just an excuse to speak to him, and she had to refrain from that. Later on, however, while making notes for her day report, the door opened and Peter walked in. He gave her a wan smile.

'Laura, sorry I haven't been in touch earlier. Please accept my apologies again about yesterday.'

She smiled back. 'Please, Peter, it doesn't matter.' She thought something like a small expression of pain crossed his face, but hurriedly concluded that it was her imagination. 'Have you heard about the charity concert Miss Hedley is giving for us?' she asked, boldly changing the subject.

To say his brow darkened would have been an understatement. 'Yes, very laudable,' he replied briefly. 'Now, I really came in to give you a copy of the patients' list for Theatre on Tuesday afternoon. There are two for us; I've yet to make a decision on the rest. I may have to do those nearer the end of the week, depending on how they are. Some of these new ones are in pretty bad shape.'

*   *   *

Word spread quickly about the concert, and it soon became clear that the charity performance was creating a great deal of interest, not to mention publicity. Also Miss Hedley announced to the Press, and the Duke himself, that she wished to visit the younger patients at the Lodge before leaving for London. The Duke and the rest of the hospital committee were delighted, and hurried plans were put into operation to receive the famous celebrity.

That night Laura found it difficult to sleep, her mind going over the day she had spent with Peter again and again. The happiness and delight they had found in each other's company, without reference to the night of the party, when they had gone back to his flat, had added a new dimension to the bond between them. Was all of that to be forgotten?

With a small groan of despair she knew she had definitely fallen in love with him, despite her subconscious reminding her what a fool she was. How quickly he had changed on seeing this other woman. Maybe he had contacted her at the theatre and said he was working at the Lodge and wanted to see her? Perhaps this was what the charity concert was really about? It was an unkind thought, but if the two had once been in love, or still were, wasn't it obvious that one or the other would make contact? Miss Hedley might even have discovered that Peter was at the Lodge before she had ever set foot in the UK. A woman in love would do anything—a man too, if he felt the same way.

A fresh tide of misery swept over her as she thought of the following day and all the honour being accorded to this person. It was almost impossible not to think that she had not planned this scheme for charity alone. Laura would never forget in the whole of her life Peter's reaction when he'd first seen her on that terrible night. Tomorrow, she wondered, would he be the same?

In Reception next day flowers had been banked hurriedly to receive Rosamund Hedley. The Duke and Duchess, members of the hospital committee and Miss Menzies, Peter Wentworth, colleagues and several nurses all lined up to welcome the guest.

Upstairs in Hyacinth and Primrose everything was shining in readiness for the great moment. Laura had been told that Miss Hedley would visit the wards downstairs first, and would be with her in fifteen minutes. Laura went to the office and, for what seemed like the hundredth time, smoothed down the crisp tailored lines of her lilac dress, for this occasion wearing her starched cap, and unnecessarily pushed back a wisp of hair from the front of her ears. Heart pounding, she went into Primrose, where Gemma and Pearl were looking just as nervous, their uniforms looking smartly efficient, and seeming to complement the flower-filled ward.

The party arrived, Miss Hedley looking even more beautiful than Laura remembered her on stage. Chic and expensively dressed, carrying a small bouquet, and flanked by two doctors on either side of her, she was introduced to the staff by Peter, Laura catching a drift of expensive perfume as the magnificent eyes shone into hers.

'I am so privileged all of you to meet.' The voice was huskily fascinating, the broken English more so. She laughed up at Peter as she spoke, but his face remained stony, rigid, as if he could not allow himself to soften in the presence of this woman who had moved him so much, as well as the crowd of people milling around her. They stopped at each bedside, Miss Hedley's face quite genuinely sad on taking a peep at little Marie and the sleeping Tiki.

When they stopped at André's cot, Laura noticed how the woman seemed to study his little face with great intent, glancing up at Peter when he told her his name. She gave a huge smile.

'Ah, I understand. André Ovsky.' She spoke rapidly to Peter in her own language, nodding as if satisfied now that she knew his name. Another smile at Peter, then she dropped a kiss on the baby's forehead, and in her very thick Slav accent declared soberly, 'This baby I lov. . .' Again she addressed Peter in her own language, and with a strained expression he replied fluently. Rosamund was no longer smiling.

When the time came to say goodbye, the retinue made to leave the ward. At the exit, with great panache, Rosamund extended her hand to Peter who brushed it formally with his lips, after a further hurriedly murmured, stiffly formal conversation. Then she swept out, and the regal visit was over.

By then Laura had had all her fears confirmed. Much had been said between Rosamund Hedley and Peter, enough certainly to confirm that the two had been reunited after perhaps a long parting. How it came about she would never know. Listlessly she tried to apply her mind to the rest of the day's work. The entire incident was now even more of a mystery, and with ever increasing despondency she realised that Peter's life abroad had been exactly that, and she could see now how little their brief affair had really meant to him.

Some two hours later the telephone rang. It was Peter. 'Staff?' The formal address was not lost upon her. 'I've just received a call from the heart specialist at Edinburgh; he's coming up here on the night train and wants to make an early visit to see Marie because he needs to be back for an important meeting. I know it's the day for the two major ops, but I'm now altering the time to begin the first one at two in the afternoon instead of the early morning, as originally planned.'

'Yes, I see, Mr Wentworth. I'll make sure everything here is ready for the professor.'

'Good. Fine.' There was a pause then he said quickly, 'It was good to see that Rosamund's visit is having the desired effect.'

'Yes. She didn't appear surprised to see you,' Laura said, unable to stop herself.

'No. We said sufficient, I think, to renew a contact I had with her some time ago.' His voice sounded withdrawn, remote, as if he was annoyed she'd had the audacity to speak of an incident so personal to him. 'So,' he said brusquely, 'nine o'clock tomorrow morning with the Professor, then.'

That evening she took herself off for a swim. She had to make a few decisions, and quite often swimming seemed to clear her brain somewhat. The main thing she needed now was to pick up the pieces of her pride, for her own sake. Even the thought of leaving the Lodge for a job elsewhere was not now an impossibility, but she loved it in Scotland and did not want to take such a step unless things became particularly difficult.

After half an hour or so she was on her way back to her room when she ran into Tim Hudson and Dennis, accompanied by two nurses. 'Hi, Laura,' Tim said, with his cheeky grin. 'How about joining us? We're just having a run down to the village pub. We're waiting around for old Willie Ferguson to come too. He's got a soft spot for you, you know!'

Laura glanced down at her ancient navy track-suit. 'OK, if I'm not too scruffy. . .'

'You look gorgeous, darling. . . Here's Willie; he'll tell you the same thing himself, won't you, old sport?'

William Ferguson gave them all a wide grin, and a special one for Laura. 'What's that, then? What am I missing?'

'I was telling Laura here she looks smashing, but you can do it better than I can!'

Willie beamed, his brown curly hair on his collar, round face and fresh complexion making him look very young.

'I sure will. Come on, Laura, you share my car; they're the scruffy lot; they can go in Tim's old banger!'

Laura was glad she'd accepted the spontaneous invitation. It was good to be back with a crowd again, without the need for anything more than crazy in-house jokes and good-natured rigging, laced with gossip about everyone they could think of. As the evening wore on they had a great sing-song, and despite Tim and Willie drinking only Cokes the evening was hilarious and did not end until midnight, with Willie extracting a promise from Laura that they'd meet again. She agreed airily. He even kissed her goodnight, which she hardly noticed, but was glad to get back to her room, feeling dead tired, and thankful that amazingly she really was going to sleep that night.

Nevertheless, in the ensuing days, Laura felt as if she was going through some kind of traumatic illness—one that had removed all sparkle from life, enthusiasm for work and dreams of the future. Each day would be the same with the added pain of seeing Peter, conversing with him, but still aware of a certain aloofness, so obvious when two people had gone through an experience that had seemed to promise so much, but yielded so little.

Going about her work on the Tuesday, Laura was again seriously considering leaving the Lodge. It was the last thing she wanted, and yet it was a way of removing herself from the man with whom she had to admit she had fallen so deeply in love. . . She forced her thoughts back to the ward, thinking of the professor who, following his detailed examination of Marie, had seemed very concerned and promised to be in touch with Peter as soon as possible following the results of his findings.

That afternoon Peter performed the two major ops. Being in Theatre with him, Laura had to concentrate hard. Apart from the strain Peter was under, one patient had to have a complicated gangrenous forearm removed from the elbow, the other a gall bladder and stones removed—in the middle of which the man's heart stopped beating.

The tension in Theatre was extreme, Peter suddenly stopping the running commentary he'd been giving for the benefit of the staff spectators behind the viewing panel. Fortunately, the anaesthetist, with Tim Hudson's help, attended the man and within seconds the electrocardiograph showed that the heartbeat had revived. Tim gave the thumbs-up sign to Peter and he carried on, opening the patient's bile duct.

He held out a hand to Laura. 'Tube, please,' he said, and inserted it into the aperture to allow some of the bile to run down into the duodenum. The brief emergency was over, everyone breathed a sigh of relief, and the operation was completed satisfactorily.

In the ante-room afterwards, while the patient was being returned to the ward and Theatre Sister was talking to one of her staff, Laura helped Peter off with his gown, his face drawn and tired as he suddenly sank down on to a chair, casting his rubber gloves into the bin, pushing off his cap and running a hand through his hair.

'Can I get you a cup of coffee, Peter?' Laura asked, feeling desperately sorry for him, what with the dilemma that appeared to be stalking him. She could not help herself, despite everything.

He gave her a gentle smile of incredible sweetness. 'No, you look after yourself, Laura. I'd like to see you in the common-room in about ten minutes, if that's OK.'

Once Laura had washed, and rung Hyacinth to check that Pearl had set up a bottle at the patient's bedside for further free drainage of the bile, and the amputation patient was now sleeping normally, she went along to the common-room and waited for Peter. She was parched and anxious. Having got herself a cup of coffee, she found a comfortable chair for them both in front of the window overlooking the Lodge lawns and the loch, the latter affording a metallic grey reflection of the sky.

Peter turned up in the next few minutes, carrying a tray and two cups of coffee. He gave her a wan smile, glancing at her empty cup. 'I had a feeling you'd want another!'

It was only a small thing but his consideration warmed her. It was wellnigh impossible to steel herself against him; even her body reacted as if they were one person in tune with each other's thoughts and needs. Hastily, she pushed such thinking aside, hoping that none of it was revealed in her expression. She felt listless and untidy, absently pushing back curls that *would* escape from her newly washed hair; she knew her face was pale, but it no longer seemed to matter.

Peter said suddenly, 'The news isn't good about Marie, I'm afraid, Laura. The professor rang while we were in Theatre; he still wants to discuss the results with colleagues, but the prognosis seems to be that she has developed a heart disease that means death if we can't do something almost immediately, within a few weeks or so. Our own efforts aren't enough. As he pointed out, there's only one piece of equipment that will save her, and that's in the Hospital for Children at Great Ormond Street, London.'

'What are we going to do?' Laura asked in quiet desperation.

'Well, once I've had confirmation from the professor, we'll naturally enlist his help, then get on to Great Ormond Street immediately. What sort of difficulties may lie ahead we cannot tell at this stage, but I intend talking it through with Miss Menzies this morning, and when we've heard from Edinburgh we'll decide upon the next step.'

There was one thing that cheered Laura and everyone else on that otherwise rather doleful day. In the early evening, just as Laura was planning to go off duty, they had a visitor. Ann Weekes, the original sister of Primrose, came bounding in, giving them all a huge smile, and looking vastly improved in health herself.

'Hi, everyone! It's terrific seeing you all again!' she said cheerfully, looking all around her. 'It seems ages since I've been here!'

Laura said quickly, 'It's great to see you, Ann, can we assume that Tony's really on the mend now after that dreadful accident?'

Ann nodded happily. 'Well, as you know it's been a long haul and he's spent weeks in hospital, but—wait for it—tomorrow he's coming home! Thank heaven complications we were half expecting didn't materialise after the splenectomy. At present he's just troubled with irritation of the left side of the diaphragm, which causes a certain amount of hiccuping, but we're optimistic that will right itself.'

'Oh, that's wonderful, Ann,' Dennis said warmly. 'Give him our best tomorrow, won't you?'

'I certainly will. He's so appreciative of all the

contact everyone's had with him. He firmly believes it helped him through.'

Pearl put the question they all wanted to ask but were hesitant to do so. 'When do you think he'll be able to start work again, Ann?'

'Well, the doctors are very optimistic; they think after a month's convalescence or so, and provided his regular checks at the hospital are OK, he should start with something nice and easy. You know, like feeding the pigs!'

'Not mucking them out, I hope!' Dennis quipped.

'No, I'll be doing that!' Ann laughed. 'Oh, it's so lovely to be here with you all, I can hardly believe it. Come on, now, tell me all the latest news!'

They made tea and stood in the kitchen chatting over the various things that had happened, including Rosamund Hedley's visit, and the latest sad possibility that little Marie might be leaving for Great Ormond Street.

'Poor little thing,' Ann said quickly. 'I do hope I can get back to work before she goes, although it seems unlikely. Incidentally, I've been in to see Miss Menzies and she said that when I feel I can leave Tony I can start with part-time hours, which is terrific!'

When Ann left, there was a lighter atmosphere everywhere; she was the sort of person who spread that kind of aura about her. Gemma arrived on duty, fortunately having met Ann just before she reached Reception. 'She looks great, doesn't she? We could do with her extra hands at the moment. I see from the list that old Peter has three more ops to do tomorrow. Hell, that'll be quite something if they all start yelling the minute they see an injection syringe for their pre-meds, as those two did today. Men are a queer species, aren't they?'

Pearl giggled. 'You're right there. I practically have

to chase my old man before I can get him through the dentist's door, let alone in the chair!'

It was a further two days before Peter heard from the professor, and the news was disquieting. Great Ormond Street could not possibly take another child at present for the specialist treatment; they already had a waiting list of children in a far more advanced state of heart disease than Marie. As Peter relayed this information to Laura he looked more and more concerned, at the same time idly fiddling with some linked paper-clips, which Laura was sure he hardly knew he was doing.

It was irritating to see; he had never shown such outward signs of tension before. Maybe after coping with the three ops yesterday he was reaching the end of his tether. It could be also that the knowledge that Rosamund Hedley was giving her various recitals in other main cities of the UK, finishing in London, was adding inner stress to his problems. Occasionally a picture appeared of her in the national newspapers, her tour, it seemed, a success all the way, which probably wasn't helping him. Now she heard him murmur, 'Apparently there's one other way. . .'

'And that is?' she asked, feeling she had to draw him back from his reverie.

'To get Marie to the United States. There is the equipment there at one of the children's hospitals in Southern California. Trouble is, it costs money, lots of it, because the child has to remain there for months on end, and she needs to have someone with her in the first instance. . .'

Suddenly he thumped a fist on the desk. 'Actually I know just the person. You may remember the French Red Cross nurse who came with us when we first arrived. She loved that child and if only we could somehow get the money Marie could be in her capable hands. It's just a remote possibility I could fix it if we can somehow raise the necessary.'

Despite Laura's thoughts about leaving the Lodge, for one horribly selfish moment she thought Peter was going to suggest that *she* go to California, and balked at leaving while things were so difficult between them. At least she wanted the satisfaction of going on her own decision and making up her own mind. Nevertheless, an idea was beginning to form in her head. . .

That night at the musical club, before they began, Laura called for some hush and asked Peter if he would tell the group what he had told her. Rather surprised at the suddenness of her request, he did what she asked. On conclusion, everyone was a hundred per cent determined to set up sponsors and charity events in order to get little Marie to the other side of the Atlantic. Meanwhile, they would all set to and get to work. Dennis had a good idea, too.

'Well, I would say one of the first things we should do is to contact both local and national newspapers, explaining our plight. Maybe the locals first, seeing as they so recently had us in the news with Rosamund Hedley and her generosity.'

They all agreed. A disco in the village hall at Brora for the youngsters, another at the Lodge for adults. Jumble and car-boot sales, and the rest, were suggested, and although little music was played that evening the discussion was worthwhile and gave the staff a goal to aim for. Even young Yasmin was not forgotten, because someone remarked upon the exquisite embroidery they had seen her working on since her recovery from scabies, and it was suggested that she and one or two other children organise a small sale of work under Yasmin's direction which would make her even more happily occupied.

A week later, with both the professor's and Peter Wentworth's backing, the hospital in California telephoned to say that they would be prepared to take the child and fees could be sent as and when available. Great jubilation ensued and from then on even Peter seemed to be carrying a lighter burden than before. The big project had also given Laura something to think about other than hopeless dreams.

In the swimming-pool that evening she was clambering out for a final dive when she sensed someone trying to attract her attention. It was Peter upstairs in the balcony restaurant, wanting her to go up there. She dressed hurriedly, and when she met him it was obvious he had something of importance to say.

'Tremendous news, Laura!' he burst out the minute she appeared. 'Naturally the Duke has heard of our endeavours; he and the Duchess are joining in any way they can. But even more fantastic is that if we can get organised in two days he's prepared to put his Cessna and pilot at our disposal to transport Marie to Heathrow, or at least to the outskirts, where an ambulance will be waiting to transfer her to the plane for Paris.

'I've already contacted the French nurse I mentioned and at present she's free to accompany Marie from Paris to California, and stay as long as necessary with her! She's absolutely delighted, as you can imagine!'

Laura felt a huge glow of happiness for the whole world at large. 'Oh, Peter, that's super!' she smiled. 'People are so incredibly kind!'

He loved the way her nose wrinkled when she laughed. 'So,' he said, giving the words some weight, 'you must have Marie and yourself ready by Saturday!'

'Me!' she gasped in astonishment. 'But, Peter, I——'

'I won't take no for an answer! Marie knows both of us, and we want her to feel as happy as possible on

the first leg of her journey to London. Miss Menzies
is in full agreement, the committee also. Now, do you
think you can organise things?'

'You won't see me for dust,' she laughed, eyes sparkling. 'Young Marie deserves to have her life given
back to her.'

At her words, Peter was suddenly struck by the glow
of sheer beauty on Laura's face. If only things could
be straightforward amid the welter of problems that
beset him, he thought recklessly. He knew without
doubt that he could love this girl for the rest of his
life, and yet it was not possible to give her one hint
of such a development while Rosamund was holding
his future in her hands. . .

He realised he was gazing at Laura rather too
intently. 'Yes,' he answered, as if he had hardly heard
her. 'Marie's a fighter; she'll win through. . .' His mind
was still dwelling upon the enormity of the conclusion
he had made about Laura. At long last he had admitted
it to himself and now nothing would change his
mind. . .ever, whatever the outcome.

Sharply he braced his shoulders back, like an athlete
who had suddenly seen a way through to the winning
post. This revelation threw a totally different light upon
his seemingly insurmountable problems. The fight was
on. But for a while Laura must have no idea. . .

By Saturday morning Marie had received sacks of
good-luck and get-well cards from literally the world,
through the assistance of the media, and, although she
loved her new toys, still the old toy duck was clutched
tightly to her as she waved to all the staff who had
turned out to see them leave. The brave little two-year-
old did not really understand what it was all about,
but enjoyed the attention just the same.

It took less than two hours to reach Heathrow;

after Marie was airborne, having already beguiled the stewards and stewardesses on board, Peter and Laura took a taxi to a hotel near to the private airfield from where they would later leave for the Lodge.

Now that they were alone and the pent-up excitement of Marie's emotional departure had receded, Laura suddenly felt slightly self-conscious with Peter. Yet over dinner at the hotel he was his usual charming and courteous self, acting as he always did on such occasions. They talked mostly about work at the hospital while they ate. When coffee was poured for them and the waiter gone, Peter said suddenly, 'Laura, I won't be returning with you tonight.'

She put down her coffee-cup with a small clatter, looking at him as if she'd imagined the words, then said hoarsely, 'You did say you're not coming back, Peter?' His bombshell had made her almost incapable of thinking straight. It was the very last thing she expected him to say.

He saw the bitter disappointment in her eyes, yet knew this was something he simply had to do. She looked so enchanting in the dark blue suit she wore, and his thoughts plummeted at what lay ahead. Hurting Laura was like plunging a knife into his own chest. If only things were different. . . He tried to soften his announcement. 'Well, not tonight, anyway. I have some business to attend to with Rosamund Hedley, and this trip to London is an unexpected chance to deal with it.'

She glanced away from the intense look in his eyes, hating him and loving him for giving up the few extra hours they might have spent together that evening talking things over away from the Lodge, an opportunity perhaps to bring up all the unanswered questions that had plagued her mind ever since that awful night at the concert in Inverness. Now she knew all of that had simply been wishful thinking on her part, and had to close her mind to any further childish ideas of happy endings.

She looked up at him, meeting his gaze unflinchingly, saying, 'I see; well, that's quite a good thing, I suppose. It's difficult to deal with all one's affairs from where we live, it's such an isolated spot. Pity all these lovely London shops are closed now; I might have had time for shopping!' she added flippantly, yet knowing she would not have given up his invitation to dinner for anything.

'You could have gone, instead of being here with me,' he said, with a small frown, 'although you know how much I enjoy your company.'

She looked at him from beneath her lashes. 'Me too,' she murmured. It was the only thing pertaining to the early days of their friendship she had let slip, but hurriedly she added, 'But strangely flying always makes me hungry!'

He looked at his wristwatch, the small dark hairs on his wrist flattened by the gold strap. 'Talking of which, I think it's time we got you back to the airfield. We'll take a taxi. Hopefully I'll be getting the first shuttle tomorrow morning into Edinburgh, where I intend stopping off to talk to the professor, then I'll get back to the Lodge by some other means; it depends largely upon timing.'

Laura toyed with her empty wine glass absently, then said, 'Peter, forgive me for asking, but does Rosamund Hedley mean anything to you? Is she. . .? Has she——?'

Peter broke in, feeling a brute, 'No, is the short answer,' he said forcefully. 'As I mentioned I'm having to see her on business, and that's really all I can say just now.' His eyes softened as he reached across to touch her slender hand. 'Perhaps later I might be able to tell you more, but for now the complications are too great to speculate upon the outcome.'

She shook her head. 'I'm sorry, Peter; I didn't want you to do that. It was remiss of me even to put the question to you about Rosamund.'

He leaned across the table towards her, dark eyes troubled. 'Laura,' he said in a low voice, 'at the very least we're friends. I do not see your question as an intrusion. All I long for is to straighten out this area of my life.'

And with that she had to be content.

He knew by the bewildered look in her eyes that his answer had not satisfied her, and cursed the way fate had dealt him such a hard blow. And yet, but for that, Laura of the violet eyes and beautiful face would never have entered so dramatically into his life. . .

Laura recalled little of her plane trip back; it was dark by then anyway. The outward journey had been so different, and yet all the possibilities that had crammed her mind had been figments of her imagination; they had come to nothing and she knew she must avoid falling into such a trap again.

Before going to sleep that night she thought of Rosamund meeting Peter. Miss Hedley had no doubt completed her tour and arrived back in London. Peter knew this and was, as he'd said, seizing the opportunity offered him. 'Business' was not quite the word she would have put upon it, she thought churlishly. He probably was an old lover of Rosamund Hedley's, despite what he'd told her. Through her professional travels abroad she had sought him out, knowing his fiancée had been killed, the sort of woman who would stop at nothing when she wanted something—or someone, married or not.

Laura could think of no other explanation, and it

left her heavy-hearted with misery. Sooner or later she really was going to have to come to a final decision about whether to leave the Lodge; the situation was becoming too unbearable.

Next morning on Primrose Laura was very perturbed to learn that Pearl, while doing the children's PTRs, had discovered that André appeared to have developed a high temperature. 'Oh, no. . .' she murmured distractedly when Pearl told her, knowing how Peter would respond. Hurriedly she leafed through the night-report book. 'No, he was OK during the night, it seems, and slept well too,' she told Pearl. 'Are you quite sure about this?'

Pearl nodded. 'Yes, but it might be as well for you to check this time.'

The same result was achieved. 'OK, Pearl, apply some cool compresses on his head and give him plenty of lemon barley drinks. Fortunately Mr Wentworth hopes to be back some time this afternoon.'

André slept for most of the morning, yet still tossed about fretfully. Between them either Pearl, Gemma or Laura remained at the cotside to watch out for any other signs, perhaps of abdominal pains, sickness, or even a rash. But by lunchtime the only change was that he refused to take any food.

'Well, that's not so unusual with this temp,' Laura murmured, brushing the child's damp curls back from his forehead, trying to keep calm at the thought of Peter's return.

CHAPTER NINE

PETER came striding into the office two hours later, greeting her amiably enough. 'Pretty good journey, thanks,' he said, in answer to her question. 'Breakfast was nice on the plane. The professor sends his regards to everyone, and says he'll be in touch as soon as he hears of Marie's safe arrival. Vice versa if California ring me first.' He gave her one of his studied looks of consideration. 'And how was the trip back? You're not too tired, I hope?'

The compassion in his voice made her want to burst into tears and beg him to tell her what was wrong. Did he no longer have any feelings for her at all? Was she so terribly naïve to keep hoping there was something left of their passionate affair that had been so right between them. . .? She smiled at him, remembering her sleepless night, hoping the shadows were not too noticeable beneath her eyes. 'Oh, the journey was terrific, thanks! No, I'm not a bit tired!'

He gave a small grin that could have meant anything, even perhaps denoting that he suspected her words were not entirely true. He picked up the night report, glancing through, then putting it aside. 'Everything seems to be all right in Primrose today, then?'

She took a deep breath for the moment she'd been dreading. 'André's temp is up this morning; there's no other sign of anything wrong, except that he's restless. He slept most of the morning.'

A deep frown crossed his brow. 'Have you given him anything?' he said sharply.

'Only liquid aspirin.'

He turned on his heel, went into the ward and headed straight for André's cot, briefly examining the child as Laura joined him. 'Oh, God, don't let it be diphtheria!'

Laura was amazed at the desperation in his voice. The pain on his face revealed something far beyond normal concern.

The child whimpered suddenly, then gave a sneeze, followed by a cough. Running a hand across his hot face, Peter said, 'It could be an upper respiratory infection. I thought it was too good to be true that he'd escaped so lightly without illness, except for the malnutrition. Make sure he has plenty of fluids, Laura, and later I want him put on a ten-day course of penicillin.'

She looked at Peter anxiously. 'But, Peter, don't you think we should wait for a day or two? It may only be a light cold—you know what children are like; the temp could have disappeared by morning.'

He suddenly turned on her, face gaunt. 'Staff Nurse Meadows,' he said, as if controlling himself with difficulty, 'I'd thank you not to question my decisions I make with patients. Is that quite understood?'

'Yes, Mr Wentworth, I'm sorry.'

But Laura was furious at his outburst, to put it mildly. She considered Peter's attitude overbearing and incomprehensible, especially as he seemed determined to remain at the child's bedside. When he was needed elsewhere, she took up the bedside vigil, conscience-stricken because they had other far more sick children on their hands to be watched over.

Still perplexed by the baby's intermittent sobbing, Laura noticed after a time how his chubby little fist constantly rubbed at his mouth. To think this over she went into the kitchen to make herself a cup of tea. Pearl was just about to go off duty. 'Hi, Pearl; you've never had a baby, have you?' Laura said jokily.

'Give a girl a chance, Laura! I've only been married two months; we practically married the first day we met!'

Laura grinned. 'Sorry, Pearl, yes, of course.'

'Why the question?' Pearl asked.

'Well, I've a theory about this temp of André's, but as I haven't had a baby either I would have liked confirmation of the fact that the only thing wrong with him is that he's started teething.'

'Of course! That could be it! My sister's baby had the same thing; I've just remembered.'

'Great. OK, I'm going to take a chance and give André something to ease him.'

Back in the ward, almost in silent defiance, Laura gave the child a spoonful of sweet aniseed mixture which André swallowed eventually. Then, worn out with crying, he allowed Laura to run her little finger gently along the swollen red gums. Yes, as she had thought, the two tiny sharp pinnacles of his first teeth had just split the gums, the previous lack of nutritous food and care having delayed the usual development of a baby of nearly ten months.

While André slept, Laura rang Peter and told him, to put his mind at rest, and suggested he come up to the ward. He still looked stern when he arrived, but as soon as she proved to him that André was indeed teething he ran a hand over his eyes, saying, 'Thank you, Laura. Heavens above, I must be losing my grip not to notice such a simple thing as that. . .'

He ran a hand over his jawline, as if deep in thought, then said, 'Laura, in view of this, there's something I must tell you. Will you come to my flat tonight? It's really the only place where we can talk privately when I'm on call.'

That evening Laura felt no sudden rise of excitement, or even hope, when she walked across the grounds to Peter's flat. In fact, quite the opposite. She was convinced that because of what he considered his lapse of judgement he intended telling her the ongoing story of Rosamund Hedley. Maybe that they intended renewing an old love-affair and once all present difficulties were ironed out would be married. Despite his recent denial to that effect, Laura was not aware if the woman was married or not, but assumed it would be no problem either way.

After she tapped on his door there was a slight delay. Dressed in T-shirt and jeans, she felt lifeless and unattractive as she stood waiting—rather like an agony aunt to whom people spilled out their troubles. . .

Peter opened the door, himself wearing jeans and a black polo-necked sweater. He had obviously just showered, his hair damp, springing into small curls. . . and every part of her yearned to take him in her arms. He said quickly, 'Sorry to keep you, Laura; do come in.' He ran a hand across his hair. 'Forgive the tousled look; there wasn't time to deal with that, I'm afraid!'

She smiled, almost feeling faint on entering the room where they had shared such passionate embraces. . .

'What will you have? Wine, whisky, coffee?'

'Coffee, thanks, Peter.' She wanted nothing that would stimulate the senses; the coffee would have to do.

They sat down on the settee, and she forced her brain to take in what he was saying, although with him looking so very rugged and attractive it was an almost impossible thing to do. He didn't attempt to pour the coffee, but sat staring at the carpet, hands linked together, as if trying to assemble what he wanted to say, then said quietly, 'I must thank you so much, Laura, for putting up with me as you have. I've been a difficult swine lately, I know, and today's revelation made me see that this can't go on.'

He sat back then, his expressive eyes meeting hers.
'I'll keep this as short as I can. Nevertheless, before
then, do I have your forgiveness for the way I snapped
at you earlier? I can't apologise enough for that. . .'

'Forget it, Peter.'

'OK. Well, you remember I told you of Marika's
death and that of her parents, all killed, crushed
beneath a falling building? It wasn't the full story by
any means. That building was a maternity hospital; her
parents were waiting to hear the news, for Marika
was there. . .having our baby; she was in labour at
that time. . . As you know we were to be married
shortly. . .'

His voice dropped almost to a whisper. 'When it
was learned that the building collapsed crowds of
people rushed to help; we spent all night reducing the
mound of bricks one by one, hoping to find survivors,
if any. But it wasn't to be.' His dark eyes misted over,
but he went on, 'She was very beautiful and we were
both so happy about the son we hoped to have. . .'

He stood up suddenly, his back to her, staring at a
silver-framed photograph of a lovely dark-haired girl
that Laura had not noticed until now. He seemed to
draw back his shoulders briskly, then resumed his seat
beside her.

To ease the tension, Laura poured the coffee, and
he continued in a stronger voice, 'There was just no
hope of finding anyone alive, we were told, but we
refused to believe it. As dawn broke, someone thought
they heard the faint cry of a baby; microphones were
taken down a small safety shaft that had been made.
A renewed attack on the rubble began. There we all
were, a hundred or so, both men and women working
like devils on hearing that there might still be a sign
of life amid so much death.'

He heaved a huge, deep sigh, staring into space again, seeing in his mind's eye the terrible devastation which he would remember for the rest of his life. He carried on.

'Some hours later our persistence and patience were rewarded and a tiny child was rescued from the rubble, the men returning with this warmly wrapped little bundle, one of them holding the child to him as if it was a precious symbol to everyone of new hope. The baby was rushed to hospital and I returned to my digs, desolated with grief at Marika's death and no longer harbouring any hope for a child. Later I was called on the telephone and told to report to that same hospital immediately, but, being used to that, thought nothing of it.

'In the child incubator room, the newly born rescued baby lay sleeping. I couldn't understand why there had been a certain amount of whispering as I arrived, and assumed it to be because I was on the scene when the child was found, as were many others, who will remain friends for as long as I live.

'The sister in charge had a strangely emotional look on her face, then of all things took me by the hand. . .' A smile lit his face at the memory. 'I thought the woman must be over-emotional with stress and anxiety. Yet we'd all suffered so much death and destruction, it was an everyday occurrence.

'However, I found myself standing beside the incubator where the baby lay. I nodded to the sister, saying rather impatiently, Is there anything specific you needed me for? I was exhausted, dispirited, and desperately needed a couple of hours' sleep, but while I was being so selfish Sister had opened the small porthole at the side of the incubator and was holding the baby's tiny hand—and on its wrist was a band upon which was written 'Baby Ovsky'—Marika's surname!'

Laura's mouth dropped open. 'Your baby? Yours and Marika's?' she said stupidly, not really knowing what to say at such a marvellous revelation. Then impulsively she threw her arms around Peter, kissing the side of his cheek, 'God! What a fantastic thing to happen!'

He was smiling himself now, reliving the thrill of that wonderfull moment. 'Laura, Laura, why didn't I tell you before? It's so good to talk to you about it.' He hugged her, the sheer joy of releasing the true facts making him feel terrific. 'And, just to return to the hospital again for a moment, while recovering myself with my son in my arms, Sister pointed to the parents' viewing panel, and there were some half-dozen members of staff all clapping, waving, tears and laughter on their faces. I can tell you, Laura, never had a baby had a more ecstatic welcome to the world than this one!'

Laura had completely forgotten her own feelings with the sheer thrill of Peter's revelations. Everything but the fact that his child had survived such tragedy seemed so unimportant suddenly. 'So however did you cope after that, Peter?' she asked eagerly.

He smiled broadly. 'I refuse to say any more until you help me eat some of these ham sandwiches I made before you came. We'll have fresh coffee too, then I'll carry on.'

'OK,' she said brightly, perhaps subconsciously aware that her normally happy, contented personality was returning. Maybe because he had not mentioned Rosamund, as she had been expecting? Then common sense intervened. There was still plenty of time for that lady to take her part in the story. 'This ham is delicious, Peter,' she said, surprised to be finishing every crumb, and pushing her own thoughts aside.

He grinned, beginning to look more like his old self.

'Thank you. Now, you asked how I coped with regard to the baby. Naturally he was in hospital for several more weeks; after I'd had it confirmed that no other survivors were found in the shattered building. I contacted a nursing order of French nuns whom I'd known previously when I worked in Paris. Absolutely devastated still at the loss of Marika, but so blessed as to have our child, I began to pull a few strings in order to have him placed in the care of the nuns temporarily, with a view to returning him to the UK and thereafter to my parents.

'I told no one in Paris or at the convent that André was my son, being so worried that I wouldn't be allowed to have him on the mercy plane with me. You see, I knew it was a question of priorities, but I felt that, given his narrow escape from death and the fact that he was ostensibly now an orphan, the authorities would consider him a serious contender to be removed to a place of safety. As it transpired this is what did happen, and I intended working the rest out later.

So, when I ultimately received all the necessary documents, everything seemed fine, except that I didn't bargain for a stray bullet that caught me in the chest on my way home to my apartment on foot! It was just bad luck. However, one of my colleagues stitched me up; it was a clean wound and he did what was necessary. Hell-bent as I was to get that mercy plane home with the baby three days later, just nothing was going to stop me. I had already volunteered to go as medical crew on the plane anyway, thereafter banking on the child being kept at the Lodge for a few weeks. Then I planned to take André to my parents for a while, rather praying I could eventually gain someone's confidence at the Lodge and get them to understand my predicament. . .'

Laura was almost speechless, but recovered enough

to say, 'I see. . .I see now why the child was so important to you.'

'Well, I could hardly bear him to be out of my sight when we actually began the journey with the rest of the patients. No one else on board knew about André, and I naturally had to pull my weight to care for the other children also, but——' he laughed '—feeling so weak, having refused to be hospitalised, I found it rather tricky. However, the trip being comparatively short, I survived.' He held her eyes with his in open admiration. 'Had it not been for your astute observation on that day we arrived, Laura, I may not have done.'

'And that was why you were clutching young André so possessively! It all makes sense now—your deep concern for him in general, the expressions on your face if he showed any signs of being unwell.'

'Yes. I've been living in fear of being parted from him; if he'd developed a disease of some kind and had to be transferred to another hospital, I don't know what I would have done. I shall soon be visiting my parents now with regard to their plans to have him for a while.'

But Laura's mind was still dwelling on the past weeks. 'No wonder you accepted the job so quickly at the hospital; that was something you couldn't possibly have arranged!'

'Exactly,' he smiled. 'I thought I made a pretty bad job of appearing uncertain whether I should accept the post or not. In actual fact I could hardly believe my good fortune.

'Now, about Rosamund. She is in actual fact Marika's sister. I had gathered from Marika they had never got on too well together, and although both had musical training their paths rarely crossed. On the day she gave the concert in Inverness, to say I was shocked was putting it mildly. I had no idea what she was doing, or her stage name, or progress, or anything else. I'd only met her once, when Marika and I met her by accident in Paris at a restaurant there. She was very offhand; in some ways I think there might have been an element of professional jealousy between the two, although Marika was the younger.

'Anyway, apparently she was determined to search me out when she learned of Marika's death, and the baby's—as she thought. But having then discovered that André lived, and I had taken the baby, that day at the Lodge she wrung out of me the true facts, knowing that the name Ovsky was too much of a coincidence—being her family name too—for André not to be her nephew, and indicated she would fight for the child, as Rosamund herself is the sole survivor of their family and she wants André to be part of it.'

Peter sat back suddenly, as if not so much the talking but the emotional situations he had retold had hit him again with all the underlying desperate sadness of it.

Laura's heart cried out to him. Once more all her former conclusions had been turned on their head. She said softly, 'The dilemma for you must be unbearable, Peter. Do you think Rosamund will make a claim for the baby?'

'It might have to end with a legal wrangle. I'm not sure yet; these things take a long time. However, there is one more chance, perhaps. Rosamund wants to see me again in London before she leaves for Paris. Whether she has anything worthwhile to say remains to be seen.

'I'm André's natural father and I think I have more claim upon him than her, but if it goes to law she may be able to win on the strength alone of being female, and considered more suitable to care for the child than a male with, as yet, no definite home base or family life. My aim, of course, is ultimately to take a job in Edinburgh, find a house, and arrange for a nanny to look after André.'

'When will you be seeing Rosamund?' Laura asked.

'Tomorrow. I should be back the following morning.' He stood up suddenly, drawing her to her feet, her hands clasped tightly in his. 'Thank you, Laura, for listening to all of this. Even so, I'd appreciate it for a while if you'd keep the whole thing to yourself, otherwise the Press will be down here like a shot, and that's the last thing we want at the Lodge.'

He leaned forward, brushing her smooth brow with his lips. 'I don't know what I should have done without you, you know that, don't you. . .?' His eyes held hers briefly. 'Neither have I forgotten. . .anything else that happened between us. . . Never will.'

Laura felt tears sting at the back of her eyes, threatening to reduce the calm demeanour she had so far managed, and didn't want it to be any different now, not in front of Peter anyway. She tilted her head back to look up at him, her gaze frank with understanding, and the words fell voluntarily from her lips. 'I shall be here if you need any more help, Peter, and rest assured I'll say nothing to anyone. I just hope something good comes out of the London trip for you.'

For the next two days Laura went around in a dream. Gemma, of course, noticed, and one evening invited her to her room for a cup of chocolate before bed. 'I can't say I haven't spotted you going around like Doomsday itself, love. What's happened now?'

Laura sipped her drink, trying to assemble what she could say to her friend which would not break her promise to Peter. She sighed deeply. 'Well, just nothing, I suppose. . .' she said, trying to bide for time.

Gemma shook her head in despair. 'Do you know what I think?'

Laura kept her eyes firmly on the carpet, murmuring, 'Haven't a clue.'

'Well, I think Peter Wentworth is two-timing you. You remember when we first saw Rosamund Hedley at the hospital we saw them gossiping in her language and very fluent and intense it sounded, too. To me, it seemed they had known each other for some time, perhaps when they were abroad, and despite his straight face when they were here he was pleading with her to renew their broken love-affair. After all, it wasn't long after she did that concert at Inverness that she appeared up here, was it? It probably suited her image to renew acquaintance with an ex-lover.' Gemma looked at Laura obliquely. 'He's not married, is he?'

'As far as I know he isn't,' Laura said as firmly as she could.

'What about Rosamund?'

'I've no idea.' Actually it was something she hadn't thought of seriously. Her heart sank. If Rosamund was married, it would not make his claim any easier.

'Still,' Gemma was saying, 'whether she is or not. I suppose she can soon alter that. With her looks I reckon she could pull any man she wanted.'

Laura thought it was time to draw this conversation to a close. 'Well,' she said wanly, 'I suppose we all make fools of ourselves at some time or other. It's just so difficult, working as closely together as we do.'

'I'll tell you what, Laura, try and give him the old cold shoulder; that often works. I mean, in a way that's what happened between Ken and me. As you know, once I told him I was coming up here to work, he began to show more active signs of what he felt; your help on that was great. This could be the way for you.'

'I honestly don't know, Gemma,' she said truthfully.

Gemma stretched and yawned behind her hand. 'I used to say I didn't think men were worth it. Well, I've changed my mind a bit since then. But if I were you I'd amend it slightly to *some* men are just not worth it. What about William Ferguson, the new houseman? He's always asking you to go out again, isn't he? Show Peter Wentworth that you're not putting up with his concerns any longer.'

Peter returned later that afternoon. He met Laura in the common-room, and from the seriousness of his expression Laura didn't hold out much hope of a satisfactory report. They sat over tea together, Peter saying out of the blue, 'Do you know, I never thought to ask Rosamund if she was married, and it transpires that she is?' He ran a slim hand over his forehead. 'What she wanted to tell me was that she and her husband can't have children and they want to adopt little André. . .'

His words trailed off, and he finished his tea in one swallow, eyes distraught. 'Laura, I can't sit here and feel at ease. Would you come for a drink in the village tonight?'

How could she say no? Several people came in just then, Gemma among them; she knew what her friend was thinking, but didn't care. 'Yes, OK,' she answered.

'I'll pick you up at nine this evening.'

Before she went off duty, Laura had just finished the TPRs and taken the drugs trolley round both Primrose and Hyacinth when the phone rang. It was Miss Menzies. 'Just to say, Laura, we've had news that Marie is settling in well and, it appears, gradually responding to treatment. The professor is delighted, as you can imagine, although there's still a long way to go. I haven't seen Mr Wentworth this afternoon—perhaps he's not back from London yet—but if you'd pass on the message before I give it out generally I'd be glad.'

In 'their' hostelry in the village, Laura relayed the message. Peter's eyes lit up. 'Oh, what splendid news! We must tell everyone involved in the funding!'

'Yes, I gather Miss Menzies already has that in hand.'

They talked on about work for a few minutes, but inevitably returned to Peter's problems. 'So you see, Laura,' he said, 'the fact that Rosamund has told me the full story of her domestic life now puts a rather different complexion upon it.'

'What do you think will be her next move now, then?'

'She intends returning to Paris to await any decision I may make. The velvet gloves are on at present, but I can't see that particular situation lasting. Rosamund gives me the impression of being a very stubborn and strong-minded woman. At thirty years of age she's sophisticated, happily married, rich and worldly wise. I feel she'll use everything in her power to take André from me.'

He sighed, looking into the far distance. 'I would say that whatever *I* do she's likely to turn it into a battle.'

Laura listened, then said quietly, 'But what about you, Peter; what could *you* do to make things go your way?'

He made a small grimace while dwelling upon her remark. 'Spend a lot of money on legal fees; Cart André off to some remote spot on the globe. . .'

He gave a rueful grin, running a hand through his hair. 'Quite honestly at this moment, Laura, I haven't a damned clue, but there's one thing I do know. I would never ask anyone to marry me and lumber her with what might turn into a much publicised legal case, and a whole lot of attendant anxieties. There would be a hundred and one difficulties in the way, and it's my intention, however long it takes, to start off as I mean to go on. In fact, it's that very barrier that would hold me back from any such union.'

As he spoke the words they seemed to come from someone else; they did not seem to come from his heart, Peter knew they were empty sentiments. With Laura at his side he never doubted that together they could achieve miracles. But how could he ask her to take so much on?

Laura nodded. He was a man of principle and it would be impossible to shake him from such a decision. It was a hopeless situation and one that she could take no part in, except as a friend.

When they returned to the Lodge, he thanked her again for the evening and on seeing her to the door she could tell by the closed look on his expression that his thoughts were far from optimistic.

During the next few days Laura knew there was no way she could intrude upon such a personal and filial arrangement. With the various revelations that had come to light, André himself seemed even more special to her, so unequivocally certain as she was that her love for his father was deep and enduring. But that had to be a fact known only by herself.

As they worked together with the six male patients, none of whom was up and about yet, a calm estrangement fell upon herself and Peter. No animosity, no pent-up feelings of anger about their ill-fated affair. It was as if both had come to the end of their tether in the welter of Peter's problems, and now only time would tell what the future held for him.

One evening she rang her parents. Her mother

wasn't there, but her father sounded unusually cheerful. 'You sound OK, Dad. I suppose there's no hope for you and Mum to——?'

Her father cut in. 'I never give up hope, Laura, dear, and, well, although I say it myself, she's been here more often lately and some evenings we've sat talking just like the old days. Once or twice it seemed to me she was in no hurry to leave.

'But I'm not going to raise false hopes; it's up to her if we can make a go of it again. We were happy once, Laura, as you know. It just breaks my heart to think of our little family falling to pieces like this. . .'

'I know, Dad. Well, give my love to Mum when you next see her—and love to you, of course. I'll ring again next week.'

In bed that evening, Laura felt the tiniest glow of optimism and hope about her parents. Even though her own life was being blown away, at least if things improved at home the future would not seem quite so bleak. Just lately, happiness seemed in short supply. Yet, strangely, it never was on the wards. Having seen the glow of recovery on little Tiki's face, Yasmin blooming now like a young flower in her youth, and heard fresh news from Ann that Tony's checks were satisfactory enough for her to begin arranging part-time hours she could manage at work, Laura couldn't fail to be cheered..

A week later, after Peter's morning round with Mr Lomax, who was suddenly called to another ward, Peter completed writing his prescriptions then said suddenly, 'By the way, I've arranged to go down to Edinburgh to see my parents this weekend and talk things over. I need to fill in the gaps for them. I've never had much chance to give them all the details since I came home, and I owe it to them.'

'Great idea, Peter; there's a lot to arrange when they take André.'

'Indeed, I hope it won't be too long now. Miss Menzies knows nothing of this, and she has been extremely good, but I can't go on forever saying André needs specialist care. I thought this morning how well he was looking.'

'How long will you be away?'

'A week. I'm driving down and that'll concentrate the mind wonderfully! Also I have to think out a way of explaining Rosamund's part in this.'

With Peter's absence the following week, Laura missed him terribly, Gemma, nevertheless, saying it was good for her. At breakfast one morning they talked it over. Gemma was warming to the subject.

'As I said, Laura, give poor old Willie a chance; he's crackers about you, and it's time you went out and enjoyed yourself instead of always worrying about Peter and his troubles.'

Laura gave a wry grin, trying to imagine what Gemma would say if she knew only half of Peter's difficulties. 'I'll think about it.'

'There's one of our Marie Charity dances here tonight, remember; you must come to that!'

The day wore on, with Laura's mind constantly divided between the Lodge and Edinburgh. She and Pearl had just finished tidying beds following lunch when Pearl said, almost wistfully, 'It's funny not having any visitors—you know, real ones, like members of the patients' families, isn't it?'

'Yes, I know what you mean; vicars and book ladies don't seem to be quite the same—not even the Duchess, charming though she is.'

'No letters either. I wonder if we could start some

kind of pen-pal club for them? It would help their English, wouldn't it?'

'Great idea; we could always get our old pals, the local newspaper staff, to give us a column. In fact, come to think of it, it could be suggested that anyone who writes to our patients in the first place could send a small donation to our charity drive. How about the Marie Pen Club?'

'Terrific,' Pearl grinned. 'Shall I write the letter to that nice editor?'

They were about to leave the ward when one of the recently qualified nurses brought in to help on Hyacinth said to Laura, 'Staff, the man with the forearm amputation, I've noticed him groaning a bit and holding his elbow. He's one who can't speak a word of English. I thought I'd better let you know.'

Laura frowned. 'I didn't notice that he seemed uncomfortable when we did his bed just now; maybe its phantom pain. OK, thanks, Nurse. I'll ring Mr Lomax, although it's difficult without Mr Wentworth and his language abilities; I'm not sure if Mr Lomax can help in that direction!'

When Steven Lomax arrived, he gave Laura a smile. 'This will have to be in sign language, I'm afraid.' He pointed to the other patients. 'The rest of these chaps aren't really up to doing a bit of translation for us. However, let's have a look at this twenty-year-old first.'

Having drawn the curtains, Laura removed the crêpe bandages from the man's left arm. Mr Lomax examined the stump. 'Yes, there is some very slight inflammation beginning to appear there. We'll treat it with benzylpenicillin, continuing for five days just to be on the safe side. Give him pain-killers too as he appears to be suffering.'

Laura thought this seemed rather unsatisfactory but

didn't say so, instead saying, 'Mr Lomax, how about if I get young Yasmin to speak to this man in his own language, so that we can be sure of his needs?'

Steven Lomax looked relieved. 'What a splendid idea; perhaps you'll let me know later what transpires.'

As it turned out, Yasmin, in her usual down-to-earth manner, reported that the man had a headache, as well as his arm hurting. Then she gave Laura a big smile, adding, 'He has said he knows my village and his headache will go if I talk with him many times!'

Laura laughed. 'Ah, Yasmin, I see you're up to something, but if you can help get him well again that's all that matters!'

From then on Yasmin was given permission to continue her budding friendship with the young man, who seemed to perk up a great deal and forget his aches and pains in Yasmin's presence. Their laughter rang out in the ward, and with a small sigh Laura marvelled at the way of the world and the passion that ruled it. . .

CHAPTER TEN

LAURA was heavy-hearted that evening as she went off duty; Peter was never far from her mind and she still wondered if she could be strong-willed enough to overcome the great love she felt for him.

Later she went to the sports club to meet her friends at the charity dance. Willie Ferguson sought her out immediately and danced with her most of the evening, but it gave her no thrill of pleasure at all.

'You're going to kiss me goodnight, aren't you, Laura?' Willie laughed as they walked to her room and stopped outside.

'Willie Ferguson! I thought a little bird told me you already have a girlfriend at home!'

He pulled her to him, kissing her lips firmly. 'Well, she's not here, is she? What the eye doesn't see and all that!'

His kiss left her cold, which didn't surprise her. He put his arm round her in a friendly way, giving a rueful grin. 'You're an attractive girl, Laura, but I've a feeling there's someone else on your mind!'

'Well, you doctors are paid to know such things!'

'Sleep tight then, my lovely. Don't forget I'm always around if you want me!'

In bed that night Laura wondered how things were going for Peter and what the outcome would be after discussing everything with his parents. Eventually she fell asleep, but awoke next morning aware that she had experienced some kind of dream involving Peter. She couldn't, to her irritation, remember what it was all about. Throughout the day she set her subconscious to try and recall it, but the only thing that came to her was Peter, laughing happily, with André clasped in his arms.

She went to see André in Primrose. He was chuckling and gurgling as he usually did when he saw her. She let down the cotside almost hungrily, picking him up and hugging him to her, the sweet baby-softness of him, and the incredible fact that he was a son of Peter's made her want to cry out with the bitter-sweetness of it.

She began his bath routine, and it suddenly struck her like a bombshell that quite soon now she would never see him again. The realisation caused her efforts towards a new kind of positive optimism to slump badly, but her determination for change gradually overcame the feeling and she was even more resolved to put Peter from her mind.

The night before he was due home, to her great joy he rang her from Edinburgh. 'Peter! How are you?' she asked, his voice as usual sending thrills up and down her spine.

'Fine, Laura, and you?'

'The same!' Especially now that you've rung, she wanted to say, but didn't. 'How have things gone at home?' she asked.

'Pretty well, thanks. I've had long talks with my parents, and they're a hundred per cent behind what I'm aiming to do.'

'They're prepared to take André when it's considered the right time?'

'Yes, my mother's already set a room aside for the nursery! I think it's giving her a new lease of life!'

'Well, it looks as if I'll have to ring off now, Laura. See you tomorrow. You're sure you've been OK?'

Face flushed with pleasure at his last question, she hurriedly reassured him that she had, and they rang off.

Even the weather was now firmly changing for the better, Laura thought next morning. The sky was azure from the moment she awoke and there was not a cloud in the sky. She knew that she shouldn't feel so buoyant at the thought of Peter's homecoming, but she couldn't help herself. Just hearing his voice the night before had set her heart singing.

That afternoon the sun still shone, and now that the warmer weather seemed more established doors were flung wide for the children to be put out on the lawn, some in their cots. André was in his playpen with his new blue rabbit, and Laura was surprised suddenly to see him try to pull himself up on his feet, then plop down on his bottom again. This ritual went on twice more.

She was delighted. With a laugh she lifted him out on to a rug she had spread on the grass, and with her help and encouragement André took his very first baby steps.

Unbeknown to her, Peter had decided to arrive back earlier than planned, and it was at that precise moment that he appeared on the ward to witness the scene.

As he stood there by the open doors, such a great rush of love went over him, one that he had been forced to hold back for so long, that he was rooted to the spot, as if mesmerised. Until Laura seemed to sense his presence. As soon as she saw him her lovely, laughing face revealed the sort of welcome he had thought never to witness. 'Laura! Hi!' he said, moving forward. 'If I'd had a camera at that moment, seeing you with André, it would have been one of the best shots I'd ever taken!'

'Peter, you're back early!'

He picked André up in his arms, holding him high above his head as the baby chuckled, and Laura's brain at that same moment registered the small scene as being the very one she had seen in her dream, and could hardly believe it.

Peter was saying to the child, 'Yes, you young rascal! You're walking for Laura, eh? Now I want to see you doing it for me!' Just briefly they each took a chubby little hand, and André performed two more wobbly steps until he sat down with a bump again. The two of them caught each other's eye as they laughed over the baby's head, not wanting to break the moment.

Peter thought he had never seen Laura looking so beautiful, with the sunshine creating a soft gold nebulous light around her head, those violet eyes shining as he'd never seen them do before. Impulsively he said, lowering André gently back into his playpen, dropping a kiss on his head, 'There's rather a lot I want to tell you, Laura. Would you be able to come over to the flat tonight about eight?'

Laura said, 'Yes, I can easily pass up the music club tonight.' She replied coolly, knowing that Gemma would have told her to say no, but she couldn't; even if their entire conversation was to be about his Edinburgh trip, she simply had to go.

'That's great,' he smiled. 'See you later, then. I must get a shower now; I feel filthy.'

She watched him walk away, despite his words his tall, athletic figure immaculate in a beige lightweight suit she had never seen him in before, and guessed that he might have done more shopping while he was away.

That evening, taking a shower herself, later blow-drying her hair, she could hardly believe she would be spending some time with Peter, and felt strangely numb. All the tingling excitement seemed to have deserted her and she assumed it to be, on the whole, because of the brainwashing job she had done, perhaps rather too well.

She put on a new blouse, one bought weeks ago in Brora when her hopes had been high with regard to Peter and herself. It was a soft violet-blue, long-sleeved and bordering on sheer, the draped neckline low enough to give her the morale boost she desperately needed. Her skirt was slim-fitting, in a pale stone colour, shoes the best she had in a similar shade—all of which she hoped would keep her confidence from flagging while Peter told her of his plans. She brushed her hair down to her shoulders, its softly curling tresses going the way it wanted; a spray of perfume and that was it.

'Come in, Laura. . .' He opened the door to her, casual trousers and checked shirt enhancing the innate rugged, but huggable, height of him. He led her into the sitting-room. She couldn't bring herself to sit down on the settee, as it brought back memories she would rather not recall. She stood looking at him for a brief moment then perched on the arm.

He smiled at her. 'Let me get you a drink. What's it to be?'

'A fruit juice, I think, please.'

He made no comment at the choice, and had the same, placing the glasses down on the magazine table, not touching her. She looked up at him; he was standing over her, appearing to arrange his thoughts in order to tell her about the trip. She wished he would sit down a few yards from her so that she didn't have to endure the closeness, the warmth, the vibes of him, which seemed to reach out and envelop her.

Sheer panic filled him. She was so beautiful. Supposing she didn't feel the same way as he. . .? The suspense was agonising. He began telling her of the plans his parents were making, but all the while he wanted to fold her in his arms, tell her his innermost thoughts.

After a few minutes he started to stride about the room, as if the worst was still to come. Laura's hopes for a reasonably calm evening plummeted. Then, quite suddenly he broke off in mid-sentence, and crossed the room to her.

'Laura,' he said gruffly, 'can I ask you a question?'

She gave a half-grin, hoping to ease the seriousness of his expression over whatever it was he wanted to say.

'Well, you've asked me a few in your time; I don't think I've refused before, even if it was the wrong answer!'

'Will you marry me?'

She stared at him, the numbness there again, and quite literally could not speak. What a fool, imagining he'd asked her to marry him. . . A small whisper eventually filtered through. 'You did say *marry* you, Peter? If it wasn't a joke, I'm afraid I don't understand, after we discussed all your difficulties.'

He shrugged despairingly. 'How can I expect you to?' He placed a tender hand on her shoulder. 'Look, won't you sit down more comfortably?' She did as he asked. As he sat beside her, he continued, 'Forgive me for putting such a question to you; I just had to ask, despite the talk we had about so many disadvantages.'

He touched her gently on the cheek. 'But the point is, Laura, the heart is no respecter of legalities and suchlike. While I was away, I could think of nothing else but us. You see, I've loved you for far longer than you realise. But believe me, I do understand your not wanting to become involved with my life, which seems so complicated. Please forget it now. I know we'll always be good friends, which I treasure deeply. . .'

He gave a huge sigh, then a gentle smile. 'Perhaps

it was just a dream the whole time, and I must take the blame for what actually happened between us.'

'Hang on, Peter,' she said, bewildered. 'I can't take this in. Just now you said you loved me. . .I mean, that's something totally different. . .' Her heart was pounding fit to burst, her breathing erratic, her words almost incoherent.

'Laura,' he was saying in that deep, wonderful baritone, 'if I'd had even the smallest speck of doubt—which I don't—it flew out of the window when I saw you this afternoon with André. The vision of you taking him through the very first steps of his young life was a joy to see, and confirmed everything I've loved about you for so long. Even without André, my darling, your kindness, thoughtfulness—oh, there are so many other things which, as I came to know you, attracted me more deeply each day. Yet, as my love for you grew, so did my apprehension once Rosamund appeared on the scene. And——' he stroked her hair tenderly '—now I realise that living without you would be to have no sun in the sky.'

'My darling,' she whispered, hesitantly, almost shyly, still sitting as if mesmerised, unable to move, until he folded her into his arms and his lips met hers, and at last both were able to give full vent to the yearnings they had both endured for so long. . .

She moved slightly, looking up at him. 'Don't let me wake up if this is a dream, Peter, and if it isn't, will you please ask me that question once more?'

'Gladly, sweetheart,' he agreed, happiness obvious in the low tremor of his words. 'My love, will you marry me?' He'd cupped her face between his hands, eyes intent on hers, as if searching her very soul for the reply he longed to hear.

'Peter, I will marry you, and shall love you forever.'

Joy filled them on that solemn yet fantastic declaration to each other. 'Laura, we'll be so happy, I just know it. It was always intended that we should come together, right from the very beginning.' He shook his head, disbelieving. 'To think I was contemplating having to go through life without you. . .'

Their kisses were a calm, studied adoration of each other after so much unhappiness. Passion could wait, they both knew that, and in this new-found bliss wanted only to be together, touching, talking, making plans for the future. . .

'We're going to be fine, Laura, no matter what the future holds.' Love strong and true shone in his eyes as he murumured anxiously, 'You do realise that in agreeing to this marriage there's still much to be done, my darling?'

She looked up at him with a sweet smile, then leaned her head on his broad shoulder. 'For a start, my love, with two of us working on what we have to do, we halve it immediately. Nothing can ever be as bad again now that, if necessary, together we can fend off the whole world.'

'My sweet.' He kissed her again, neither wanting to break away, then glanced at the bedroom door. She knew exactly what he was thinking. 'Darling, we must be hellishly sensible while we're still at the Lodge. . .'

They kissed again with the controlled passion that would be so hard to contain. . .'My God, Laura,' Peter murmured, kissing her eyes, running his lips across the contours of her smooth cheeks, 'it's going to take years and years—forever, in fact—to tell you how much I love and want you. But we have to find a way before then!'

He smiled, eyes crinkling, brimming with happiness and the knowledge of the new world opening up to them both. 'I honestly can't believe this is happening myself now, Laura. When I knew I had to ask you if you would marry me I was so beset by fears of your refusal I just couldn't sleep. After all, why should you be interested in a man with a young baby and a near sister-in-law who seems hell-bent on making her affairs public to the media? But you know, seeing you this afternoon helping little André take his first steps, I knew that if I couldn't have you I wanted no one.'

She gazed at him, his dark eyes fixed on her face with an expression that sent a sweetly sensuous languor sweeping through her body. 'Would it make sense if I said those are exactly my thoughts about you, Peter? Where applicable, I mean.' She laughed, a delightfully joyful sound that was music to his ears.

Eventually they had to say their goodnights, and as she went up to her room she realised that the only thing Peter had said regarding their future plans was that he would be seeing Miss Menzies next morning to let her into the story of André's existence and who he really was. Everything else had been temporarily forgotten in their new-found happiness.

On the ward next day Laura did her best to concentrate, but to say she was in a dream was to put it mildly. Peter's proposal of marriage was far and away beyond anything she could have visualised, even in her wildest flights of fancy. Nevertheless, she had to remember that Rosamund was still going to be the stumbling-block for what could be several more years to come yet. But even that problem was minimal in comparison to Peter loving her. That morning she knew she had a glow about her like a beacon announcing the fantastic news to the world. . .

Her blissful reverie was cut short suddenly by the strident buzzing of the telephone in the corridor.

Laura felt sure it would be Miss Menzies, and her heart started to beat fast with anxiety. Supposing the SNO was annoyed with Peter's plan that had kept

André near him for so long at the Lodge? Supposing, too, she was displeased that two members of her specialist team were intent upon carving out a new future for themselves? After all, Laura didn't know a lot more about Peter's future intentions herself. But then, how could he plan a future with this legal tangle over André? It was impossible to make too many firm plans as yet. The only world-shattering thing Laura did know was that she and Peter loved each other and they were prepared to go through anything so long as they were together.

With great trepidation she answered the phone. The reply was curt. 'Staff, would you come down to my office immediately, please?'

As Laura replaced the receiver her heart sank. The formality that had come over did not bode well. Swiftly she told Gemma she was going down to the office, then sped downstairs because it was quicker than the lift, and tapped at Miss Menzies' door. 'Come in.'

When she entered the room, rose colour swept her cheeks as she saw Peter, a loving smile on his face, rising to his feet as Miss Menzies indicated an empty chair, her expression not exactly serious, but not joyful either.

'Good morning, Laura.' Laura's heart calmed down then. Peter was at her side once more and nothing else mattered in the whole world. 'First I want to say how very delighted I am at the news. Peter has told me you intend getting married as soon as possible.' Miss Menzies gave a brilliant smile, as if she too knew only so well what it was to be in love, and in fact Laura recalled the night of one of their dances and the distinguished-looking man with whom Miss Menzies had spent the entire evening. Maybe she was expecting the similar wonderful words that Laura had heard from Peter.

'Having said that,' Miss Menzies went on, a slight frown on her face, 'I am rather concerned for you both with regard to claiming André. I think it's a wonderful thing that Peter has done so far, and now it seems to me that you both need some positive help from outside—after, that is, you've had a straight talk with Rosamund. So this is what I suggest. . .'

One hour later, Peter and Laura were seated in the common-room before going on duty, the place empty, enabling them to talk freely. Peter grinned happily, taking Laura's hand. 'You can guess its only going to be a matter of hours now before everyone knows, but how could I ask Miss Menzies to keep it to herself when she's been so wonderfully accommodating?'

'I know, darling; she's certainly a friend of ours. Just think, though, once we've organised the tickets we'll be flying off to Paris tomorrow to see Rosamund. I have a feeling this is the last thing she expects.'

'As we said, it's probably best this way, and we may get down to the real facts much sooner. Anyway, darling, the thing is, whatever the outcome when we get back we'll contact our respective parents, then concentrate upon us!'

'I'm in such a daze, Peter, with so much happening at once. Did Miss Menzies suggest we leave André here while we're away?'

'Yes, she more or less told me before you arrived that he could stay for as long as we want him to. She intends putting the committee in the picture, so there should be no problems.'

'Great.' Laura glanced at the wall clock. 'Oh, Lord, I'm afraid I'll have to go, Peter. I really must get back to do the dressings with Pearl.'

He nodded and pressed a kiss upon her cheek. 'You look ravishing this morning, Staff Meadows!' he laughed teasingly. 'Just make sure no one else asks you to marry them between now and when I see you next! I'm going to ring the airline about our tickets in a minute. We'll leave tomorrow, if possible. Is that OK with you?'

Laura touched his face shyly, loving him to distraction. 'Marvellous! I'm even determined to feel optimistic about confronting Rosamund, if necessary!'

'Good girl! I love you, sweetheart. I'll ring you as soon as I have everything fixed up.'

Later the following night they arrived at Heathrow, booking into a nearby hotel—in separate rooms—to catch some sleep for a few hours before rising at dawn for an early flight to Charles de Gaulle airport. Having landed, they took a taxi to a small hotel near the Opera House. Peter looked concerned as they drew up outside a small, unpretentious-looking building. 'Sorry, Laura, it was the best I could do in the limited time.'

She smiled. 'None of that matters, Peter. With luck, who knows? We might be back at the Lodge tomorrow.'

'The day after, hopefully.' He smiled wryly.

They went up to their rooms, and after the bags had been delivered Peter checked that he had his room key. 'I'll just go and ring Rosamund and try to pin her down to a time.' He looked detached suddenly, withdrawn, as if this was the beginning of a harrowing duty he had to perform.

In her room, Laura was hanging up her suit before taking a quick shower when Peter returned, tapping at the door, coming in and closing it behind him. The cloud had gone from his expression as he said, 'It's OK. We're meeting at the Ritz tonight; she and her husband have an apartment there.'

'Was she surprised when you rang?'

'No, I don't think so; she was probably expecting it.'

He took a stride across the room, as if suddenly noticing that she was standing in her pink satin briefs and bra, which enhanced her slim figure to perfection. They kissed as if about to part forever. . .'Oh, my God, Laura, I won't be able to stand this much longer. Let's leave as soon as we can.'

That evening, having seen Rosamund billed at a concert hall across town, they decided to attend her recital before meeting up with her and her husband at the Ritz for dinner. Joining the theatre-going crowds, they settled in to the concert hall, where seats were filling rapidly. When Rosamund entered, taking her place in front of the full orchestra, Peter held Laura's hand tightly, and continued doing so throughout. Such were their deeply passionate feelings for each other and the joy of their life to come that although the music was magnificent it seemed a mere background for Laura and Peter, who had far more profound things on their mind, the most important just then being their great longing to establish that André would be brought up by them as their very own son.

Afterwards the fresh air was dry and a faint perfume of spring blossom hung in the atmosphere as they took a taxi to the hotel. When they arrived at the opulent magnificence of the Ritz, Laura felt her first pang of nervousness. As if knowing, Peter took her arm, and they were escorted to the Espadon Grill where Rosamund and her husband awaited Peter. But when Rosamund, exquisitely gowned as usual, saw Laura a frown crossed her beautiful face.

'This is Laura, Rosamund, Laura Meadows. She's a nurse at the Lodge where you first saw André.' Peter said.

Rosamund glanced swiftly at her husband, Pierre, as if she needed his support. A quiet man, he simply smiled with an expressive gesture after all the introductions were made, his composure seeming to calm Rosamund as he took her hand. 'It is good to meet you, Laura. I am happy that we have your company tonight.'

Peter did not intend wasting any time. He said, as soon as they were seated at the dinner table, 'Laura is my fiancée, Rosamund.'

He couldn't have made more of an impact if he had hurled a grenade in their midst. Rosamund's face was ashen suddenly. Laura felt quite sorry for her as the woman said, with a hand at her throat, 'You mean. . . you mean you are to marry Laura?'

'As soon as possible.'

Pierre was obviously very concerned as he looked at his wife, and spoke to her rapidly in French.

She shook her head. 'No. . .no. I am good. . .I am well.'

But Laura noticed that her hands were shaking; Rosamund had obviously sustained quite a shock at the totally unexpected news. She stood suddenly, swaying a little against her husband's supporting arm. 'Please forgive me; do finish your dinner. Pierre, you must rejoin Peter and Laura, then we shall all meet up again in our room when you are ready.'

On entering Rosamund's room, with its pale blue satin décor, they found her resting on a small day-couch. Colour had returned to her face and she had obviously overcome the initial trauma of hearing Peter's news about his marriage. Great tension was obvious between them all, and Laura was by now decidedly apprehensive as to the outcome of their mission.

After seeing that they were comfortably settled and Pierre had poured drinks for them, Rosamund gave them a tired smile; her piano recital, too, must have been a testing performance, Laura thought, and now it seemed she was about to give another.

'You knew you were going to marry Laura when you spoke to me at the hospital, Peter?' she asked.

'No. There was no question of it. I had many worrying things on my mind. My parents, for a start. They intended caring for André until I got a job and a home. After that. . .only time would tell.'

Rosamund had tears in her eyes. 'Marika was my lovely sister and she died,' she explained to Laura. 'My parents also, Laura, in that terrible tragedy. I am the only Ovsky left; perhaps as a woman you will understand that I will 'ave no children, so I wanted little André for my own. . .'

Laura murmured softly, 'I do understand, Rosamund.'

'But. . .' Rosamund paused briefly, taking her husband's hand as he sat protectively at her side '. . .I think that you and Peter are very happy. I can see it in your eyes, yes?'

Peter nodded, as if still wondering what exactly Rosamund was about to say. He wished she'd get on with it. He'd never really liked the woman. On the other hand, he hardly knew her, and wasn't she the sister of the woman he had loved, who had lost her life bearing his child?

'Yes, Rosamund, you are quite right. Laura and I do love each other very deeply. We also both love André. As I said, we are to be married shortly, and——'

Rosamund broke in suddenly, dabbing her eyes with a wisp of lace. 'And you would wish our blessing on that marriage, and that I do not try to adopt the dear little boy. Yes?'

'Yes, Rosamund, that's what we want more than anything else in the world.'

She nodded; she and her husband had a further conversation then as he put both arms around her and kissed her forehead. 'My Pierre and I know what it is to be in love, and we are very much glad that you are to marry Laura, Peter. Little André will now have a proper home with a mother and father who belong to him. Only the best is good enough for him. There is just one big thing I must 'ave.'

Laura's heart seemed to miss a beat as she saw Peter's jaw tighten. Rosamund smiled suddenly. 'I want you will allow Pierre and I to be the best aunt and uncle there is. That is all we wish now. You will let us do that, yes?'

Peter and Laura's anxiety visibly fell from them. Reassurances were given all round, and eventually, on saying their farewells, Laura and Peter promised to send Rosamund and Pierre an invitation to the wedding, so they would meet again very soon.

The following day, having taken an early flight back to Heathrow, they rang Laura's parents, who happened to be at home together. On hearing Laura's news they sounded overjoyed. They both spoke to Peter about coming up together for the wedding and Laura was ecstatic as they hurried to catch the shuttle for Edinburgh.

As they emerged into the arrivals hall at Edinburgh airport, so free of all the rush and bustle of Heathrow, Peter suddenly said with a glad cry, 'There they are, my darling! I rang my parents last night to arrange this; they're longing to meet you.'

At the barrier Laura saw almost an exact replica of Peter—a tall, distinguished, silver-haired man with a twinkling smile. His wife, petite, attractive and hardly able to contain her excitement at seeing them both, ran forward to greet them.

Peter introduced Laura with loving pride in his voice. 'My future wife, Mum. . . Dad. . .'

Together they went to a nearby hotel and talked as if they had known each other forever, both Jim and Susan Wentworth obviously delighted at their son's choice. 'If only you could come home with us now,' Susan said longingly. 'But you must both come to stay for a few days later on, my dears. We have so much to catch up on!'

Peter took Laura's hand. 'You'll be coming up to see us before then, darling. We're getting married as soon as possible now that Rosamund's turned up trumps!'

His father nodded approvingly. 'Quite right too, and then later we can really get to know our new grandson as well as our daughter-in-law!'

Eventually, Peter and Laura took their leave of the two, collected his BMW from the car park and set off for home. The drive was a good one and traffic quite light. They stopped several times for a snack, then eventually approached Inverness. Laura suddenly noticed that they were heading for the town centre. 'Peter, shouldn't we have taken that other turn-off?'

He grinned. 'Normally, yes, sweetheart, but tonight I think we owe it to each other to have some time alone together, before getting back to the Lodge.'

They drew up outside one of the hotels they had admired the first time they had visited Inverness together, Laura relaxed and blissfully happy at Peter's decision. The ambience of quiet restfulness and deft, smiling service in the dining-room was something they would remember forever. Coffee was served in one of the small rooms from where romantic tunes from a piano reached them, yet they were alone.

Briefly they touched upon the honeymoon, future jobs, house purchase, all of it like a wonderful dream that seemed to defy any practical discussions. Peter was simply admiring her with all the intensity of a man unable to believe he had actually been given that second chance of great happiness they had once talked about. 'Laura,' he said, the low voice deep and caressing, 'you are happy about us? You never have any thoughts about the airline steward boyfriend you told me about?'

She gave a light, rippling laugh. 'Oh, darling, that was all finished and done with when I first came up to the Lodge!'

'Thank heaven for that.' He took her hand, pressing it to his lips once again, and Laura was intensely aware of that same flare of chemistry between them which had existed almost from the very first time Peter and she had touched.

'Peter,' she whispered lovingly. 'Shall we go upstairs now?'

In their room he drew her into his arms, the slim, tantalising curves of her body pressing against his strong muscular frame.

'My darling,' he murmured, 'the last time—in fact the first time—we made love, I so wanted to tell you then how much I loved you, wanted you for the rest of my life, yet it seemed then that we had very little going for us. I knew all that, but you, of course, my sweet one, had no idea. I just couldn't inflict so much uncertainty upon you; so much that you could not possibly know about me.

'Also, of course, once Rosamund appeared on the scene it seemed inevitable that she would make some demands upon me when she knew who André was.'

He kissed her face with a shower of soft, gentle kisses. 'You too, when we made love, said that you were vulnerable on that occasion. Now tell me that it's no longer that. It's that we love. . .adore. . .'

Swiftly Laura placed a slim finger against his lips. 'My sweetheart, I shall be yours for the rest of my life; the only thing I'm vulnerable to now is you and the devastating effect you have upon me!'

He drew her more tightly to him. 'You little temptress! That's how I saw you then, and that's how I shall always see you now! My eyes will be dazzled by you for the rest of my life, my love, and when we are married we shall be as one for the rest of time.'

They were ecstatic with the brilliance that seemed to surround them, and they shook with laughter when they realised they were to sleep in a huge four-poster bed. But suddenly the reality of their commitment to each other struck them, and at long last the moment they had waited for for so long was here.

As if to underline it, their telephone rang suddenly. It was Miss Menzies, who had been the only one Peter had told they were staying in Inverness overnight. 'Peter,' she said brightly, 'did everything go reasonably well in Paris? Forgive me intruding this way, but I just had to know!'

He smiled, putting an arm around Laura's shoulders and drawing her to his side. 'Even better than we'd expected, Miss Menzies! You'll understand when I say Laura and I have agreed there could be no better place than the Lodge to hold our wedding!'

'Oh, my dears, that's terrific! The Duke has already told me that if all goes well with you the marriage service can be held in the tiny chapel here on the estate, so we shall start getting the white ribbons out now!'

Miss Menzies talked to Laura too. Everyone back at the Lodge, she said, was hoping against hope that all would go well for them. Miss Menzies chuckled suddenly. 'Can I hand you over to Gemma just for a moment? She's longing to have a word or two. . .I'll come back to you.'

'Hi, Laura! I just had to say how thrilled I am the way things have turned out! I can understand now why you didn't tell me too much! Give my love to Peter, and love to you too. See you at the wedding!'

'That's her ration, Laura,' Miss Menzies laughed. 'now we won't trouble you any more, See you both tomorrow.'

'What a lovely lot they are, 'Laura murmured, replacing the phone, 'and how lucky we are, darling.'

Peter said softly, with a wicked twinkle in his eye, 'Even so, I think we'll dispense with any further calls this evening, don't you, sweetheart? I'll just ring Reception and tell them so!' Then he drew her towards him, saying, 'This night is ours, my love. . .'

'Now and forever. . .' Laura whispered, melting into his waiting arms.

Christmas Journeys

4 new short romances all wrapped up in 1 sparkling volume.

Join four delightful couples as they journey home for the festive season—and discover the true meaning of Christmas...that love is the best gift of all!

A Man To Live For - Emma Richmond

Yule Tide - Catherine George

Mistletoe Kisses - Lynsey Stevens

Christmas Charade - Kay Gregory

Available: November 1995   **Price: £4.99**

MILLS & BOON

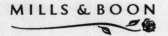

Available from WH Smith, John Menzies, Volume One, Forbuoys, Martins, Tesco, Asda, Safeway and other paperback stockists.

MILLS & BOON

CHRISTMAS CRACKERS

A cracker of a gift pack full of
Mills & Boon goodies. You'll find...

Passion—in *A Savage Betrayal* by Lynne Graham

A beautiful baby—in *A Baby for Christmas* by Anne McAllister

A Yuletide wedding—in *Yuletide Bride* by Mary Lyons

A Christmas reunion—in *Christmas Angel* by Shannon Waverly

Special Christmas price of 4 books
for £5.99 (usual price £7.96)

Published: November 1995

Available from WH Smith, John Menzies, Volume One, Forbuoys, Martins,
Tesco, Asda, Safeway and other paperback stockists.

MILLS & BOON

Kids & Kisses—where kids and romance go hand in hand.

This winter Mills & Boon brings you Kids & Kisses— a set of titles featuring lovable kids as the stars of the show!

Look out for
The Santa Sleuth by Heather Allison
That's My Baby by Caroline Anderson
in November 1995 (Love on Call series).

Kids…one of life's joys, one of life's treasures.

Kisses…of warmth, kisses of passion, kisses from mothers and kisses from lovers.

In Kids & Kisses…every story has it all.

Available from W.H. Smith, John Menzies, Volume One, Forbuoys, Martins, Tesco, Asda, Safeway and other paperback stockists.

GET 4 BOOKS AND A MYSTERY GIFT

Return this coupon and we'll send you 4 Love on Call novels and a mystery gift absolutely FREE! We'll even pay the postage and packing for you.

We're making you this offer to introduce you to the benefits of Reader Service: FREE home delivery of brand-new Love on Call novels, at least a month before they are available in the shops, FREE gifts and a monthly Newsletter packed with information.

Accepting these FREE books and gift places you under no obligation to buy, you may cancel at any time, even after receiving just your free shipment. Simply complete the coupon below and send it to:

MILLS & BOON READER SERVICE, FREEPOST, CROYDON, SURREY, CR9 3WZ.

No stamp needed

Yes, please send me 4 free Love on Call novels and a mystery gift. I understand that unless you hear from me, I will receive 4 superb new titles every month for just £1.99* each postage and packing free. I am under no obligation to purchase any books and I may cancel or suspend my subscription at any time, but the free books and gifts will be mine to keep in any case. (I am over 18 years of age)

2EP5D

Ms/Mrs/Miss/Mr _____

Address _____

_____

_____ Postcode _____

Offer closes 31st May 1996. We reserve the right to refuse an application. *Prices and terms subject to change without notice. Offer only valid in UK and Ireland and is not available to current subscribers to this series. Readers in Ireland please write to: P.O. Box 4546, Dublin 24. Overseas readers please write for details.

You may be mailed with offers from other reputable companies as a result of this application. Please tick box if you would prefer not to receive such offers.

MILLS & BOON

By Request

Bestselling romances brought back to you by popular demand

Don't miss our December title...
Just Add Children—the perfect
mix for a spicy romance!

Two complete novels in one romantic
volume by **Catherine George** and
Emma Goldrick.

Available: December 1995   Price: £3.99

*Available from WH Smith, John Menzies, Volume One, Forbuoys, Martins,
Tesco, Asda, Safeway and other paperback stockists.*